Scales and Scars

Volume 1

Gary Saurage

Dedication

This book is dedicated to my daughter, Callie; my son-in-law, Damon; and, most of all, my wife, Shannon, for believing in me and insisting that I write this story.

I would also like to dedicate this book to the people of Southeast Texas, who helped me rebuild Gator Country three times after floods and hurricanes. None of it would have been possible without their support.

Acknowledgment

Callie has always been strong. She was a wonderful child to raise—never any trouble, always incredibly athletic. She's been by my side through thick and thin, and we've always shared a close bond as father and daughter. For many years, Callie has been dedicated to Gator Country. She now manages the Alligator Park in Beaumont, Texas, and does a fabulous job.

Callie married Damon, my loyal son-in-law, who has stood with me for many years. He has also done a wonderful job at Gator Country, supporting me through the hardest times.

Then there's Shannon, my wife. We've been together for ten years, and the time has flown by. Shannon has always believed in me and in everything I've tried to accomplish. She fought for Gator Country and helped grow it into two additional alligator parks—one in Natchitoches, Louisiana, and another in South Padre Island. She has always been incredibly dedicated and loyal, and I would not have written this book without her.

About the Author

Gary Saurage has been a dedicated conservationist for over two decades. He has led the way in Texas as a nuisance alligator hunter, catching thousands of live alligators. Gary set the world record for the largest alligator ever caught alive. The alligator, named Big Tex, measured 13 feet 8½ inches and weighed 1,000 pounds—a national record for live captures.

Gary was featured in his own television series, Gator 911, which premiered in 2010 on Country Music Television. He went on to appear on A&E, Animal Planet, and several other networks. Currently, he stars in Texas Gator Savers on EarthX TV.

For more than twenty years, Gary has shared his passion for reptiles, teaching millions of children and adults about the American alligator and other species. Each year, he tours the country with a live reptile show, continuing his mission to educate and inspire.

Gary is also a motivational speaker. He encourages people not to be afraid to try, even at the risk of failure, because some of life's greatest lessons come from failing. His message is simple: never give up, never quit. Surround yourself with people who care about you, and don't listen to those who say you can't achieve your dreams. Living in the United States—the greatest country in the world—you have the opportunity to chase any dream you believe in. Never let anyone laugh at your dreams.

Table of Contents

Chapter 1
The Catch That Nearly Cost My Life

The rope had slipped. I saw it fall straight through the opening, hit the water, and vanish.

That was it, that was the plan falling apart right in front of me.

There I was fifty yards deep inside a culvert, pushing a busted trash can with a live alligator in front of me, and the one thing I was counting on, the one thing that kept this from turning into a head-on fight, was now gone.

They'd had one job: drop the lasso, get the gator. That was the whole deal.

And now I was stuck in this tight, dark, nasty culvert with a 350-pound alligator that did not want to move forward. He was slamming his tail against that trash can, tearing it up. Water was exploding in every direction. I was soaked, bleeding, and couldn't breathe right. My knees were cut open from the rocks, my hands slipping on the slime, and I couldn't see more than a few inches in front of me.

And now the rope was gone.

I looked up through that little crack between the trash can and the culvert wall, hoping they were going to drop another one. Nothing yet. Just water. Just dark.

I kept pushing, inch by inch, and I knew, if that gator figured out he could turn around, that was it. That culvert opened up at the manhole. If he turned around in there, I'd be face to face with a full-grown, angry alligator in a space barely wide enough to breathe in.

I was alone down there. No backup. No second chance. Just me, a busted trash can, and a ticking clock.

That was how it all began.

And the craziest part? I hadn't even gone out there for that big alligator.

No, I'd been called out to deal with a mama gator. That was supposed to be the job. Just a straight-up, routine nuisance call. Nothing I hadn't handled a hundred times before.

See, I was the lead nuisance alligator trapper for the state of Texas. What that meant was, if somebody found a gator where it didn't belong, like a backyard, a swimming pool, or in this case, a school, they called me. And instead of putting the animal down, we relocated it to a sanctuary. I ran one out in Beaumont, it was called Gator Country.

People always asked, "How do these gators even end up in neighborhoods?"

Well, here's how: Texas is full of marshes and bayous. When it rains hard, or when storms come through, those floodwaters turn every little ditch and drainage line into a gator highway. They follow the water. That's how they end up in yards, ponds, and sometimes even parking lots.

So the plan that morning was simple: Drive down to Sabine Pass High School, catch the mama gator, gather up her babies, and be back on the road by lunch.

That was it. That was supposed to be the job.

But the day had other plans.

I remembered the call as clear as day. It was hot, one of those thick, May mornings where the humidity just sat on your shoulders. I'd gotten a call from a Texas game warden. Said they were filming a show for Animal Planet and had a situation at a local school.

He said, "Gary, I need your help. This one's serious."

I said, "What've we got?"

He said, "We've got a mama gator, eight-footer. She's nested right by the school. She's got babies. And she's been charging at kids during recess."

Now *that* was a problem.

So I grabbed my gear, loaded up the truck, and headed out to Sabine Pass.

It was a tiny little town down on the Gulf, five miles from the Louisiana line. Not much out there but marshland and mosquitoes. The school had all twelve grades in one building. That's how small it was.

And let me tell you, alligators didn't care about fences or property lines. If it flooded, if it rained, if there was a ditch or a drain, gators came through it.

I pulled up to the school and met the game warden, Mike Boone.

Mike Boone was a veteran. He'd actually retired from Texas Parks and Wildlife. Good man. Fair. Smart. Knew his stuff. He was one of the better game wardens we had out there, really good with people, always did things by the book.

But when it came to catching big alligators alive, back in those days, that just wasn't his strong suit. That's why he'd called me.

I was the guy who went in where others didn't.

So there he was, standing there in his good uniform, nice and clean, and there was a whole TV crew behind him. Animal Planet or one of those networks. And I looked at him, and he looked at me like he already regretted making the call. Like he knew what was coming and he sure as hell didn't want to be the one crawling into a culvert with a rope in his teeth.

We walked around back and sure enough, before I even saw the mama, I saw the babies. Ten, maybe twelve of 'em, little things just floating there around what used to be a nest. The mama wasn't far. I walked up to the edge of the water and gave it a splash. That's all it took. The water exploded, here she came, full charge, snapping and hissing, ready to give her life for those babies.

See, mama gators don't mess around. They are the best mothers in the reptile world. They nest once a year, lay thirty to thirty-five eggs, and have an eighty-five percent hatch rate. And they protect those babies with everything they have. Birds, fish, snakes, even other gators, everybody wants a baby gator for lunch. So mama stays close, and she stays mean.

This mama kept coming at me, over and over, but I finally got the rope on her jaw. She rolled hard, big ol' death roll, but I held on. We got her taped up, got her loaded in the truck.

Then we went back for the babies.

Now let me tell you something, catching baby gators isn't as easy as it sounds. They are fast, and they scream. That distress call brings mama back real quick if you haven't already caught her. But we got lucky. We scooped up fifteen of 'em, boxed 'em up nice and safe. That part of the job went smooth.

And here's the thing: that day was their lucky day. In Texas, nuisance gators usually had two options: get euthanized or go to a sanctuary. Lucky for them, we'd already built one: Gator Country. They were on their way there, clean water, no threats, a place to live out the rest of their days in peace.

We got the mama and her babies loaded, the crew was packing up, and I was thinking, *Alright, we're done here.*

Then the principal walked up.

He said, "That ain't our only problem."

Now keep in mind, I was muddy, I was wet, I had just wrangled a mama gator in front of a TV crew, and I was thinking—*What could possibly top that?*

He said, "We've got another one. Under the football field."

Now, I've been doing this a long time. I'd pulled gators out of ponds, ditches, swimming pools, even out of a Whataburger parking lot once. But a football field?

He took me around to the edge of the field, and there was a culvert running straight from one end zone to the other. A hundred yards long. It was the school's drainage system. He said there was a gator living in it. About five feet, he thought.

Now five feet wasn't nothing, but it wasn't the worst either. Fast, yeah. But manageable.

I looked at Mike Boone, the game warden on duty, and said, "Okay, your turn to go in."

Mike's response was quick, as if it was rehearsed, "No, Gary. I got my good uniform on today. I ain't getting muddy. That's why I called you. You're going in the hole."

And I got it. That culvert was pitch dark. It was tight. It was wet. And it stank like old hurricane water. Still, somebody had to go in.

So we started getting ready. That's when Sal Cavazos stepped up.

Sal was a friend of mine I'd met back in 2013. He came around and volunteered his time. He was actually in some of the old Gator wrestling tournaments we had back in the day. But Sal would come out after working a full day at his own job, just to help me build Gator Country. He helped build fence posts. Helped put up buildings. Helped paint signs. Sal helped with everything around the park.

And even from the start, he was pretty good with alligators. Through the years, I trained him. I got Sal real good at what he was doing. Eventually, he started running nuisance alligator calls with me.

You'll hear more about this later, but Sal wasn't just good with gators, he was real good with venomous snakes too. In fact, he was the one who trained my wife, Shannon, when it came to working with them.

That day, he brought me a square trash can. Not ideal, but it was all we had that would fit.

Now this culvert, it was round. Thirty-six inches across. That trash can? Square. Maybe twenty-six inches wide. That meant I had maybe a couple of inches of space on either side. Just enough to peek through.

I couldn't crawl. I had to lay flat in a hole full of God-knows-what, pushing a busted-up plastic can in front of me and hoping it would get me close enough to push the gator toward the manhole.

As I got ready to go in, Sal said, "Gary, don't do that. We ain't seen that alligator. We don't know if it's really five feet."

Of course, I brushed this excuse off, "Well, the principal saw it and he said it was five feet."

So I lay down and started pushing that can in.

The water was already up to my chin. I moved my head side to side just to keep breathing. It was dark, no light once you were a few feet in. There were spiders. Turtles. Floating trash from storms long past. Some of those rocks had been rolled in by hurricanes, they were sharp enough to split a boot.

Sal stayed behind me at the entrance, holding a flashlight, keeping the trash can steady while I got started.

We didn't know where the gator was. Didn't even know for sure if he was in there.

I started crawling.

The first few feet were slow. I could feel the algae slick under my hands, the grit tearing at my knees. The culvert was tight, wet, and rough. But I kept going, pushing that trash can forward, inch by inch.

And I kept thinking—*alright, if this is a five-footer, we'll manage.*

But was it?

I kept crawling.

Thirty yards in. Then forty. Still no gator. Just water and trash and black silence.

I pushed on, fifty yards, maybe sixty, and all of a sudden that trash can just stopped. Hit something solid. Wouldn't move another inch.

Could've been storm junk. Could've been a boulder. I pressed forward again, nothing. It was heavy. And that's when I saw it.

Right over the top of the trash can, through that narrow crack of light I had on either side, I caught movement.

A tail.

Thick, armored, and long. It dropped down from the top, like it had been coiled up there, and splashed off to my right.

And just like that, I knew.

This wasn't a five-foot gator.

This thing had to be at least nine, maybe ten feet. Three hundred, maybe three-fifty pounds. Easy.

And that changed everything.

A five-footer? He was quick, but manageable. You could control him, steer him if you needed to.

But a gator pushing ten feet? That was a whole different fight. That was raw power. He was stronger than me, stronger than anything I had in there. And if he got turned around, if he found just a little room, he'd fill that culvert with nothing but teeth and muscle and bad news.

And he was right there in front of me.

I was sixty yards in, lying flat in a wet culvert, water lapping at my chin, and now I had 350 pounds of prehistoric muscle boxed in with me, with only a beat-up plastic trash can between us.

I was thinking—he's blocking the culvert. That tail dropped from the top. That meant he was laying crosswise, head toward the manhole end. I had only one shot: push him forward.

But I didn't know if he could turn around.

If he couldn't, I had a chance.

If he could… then I was face-to-face with a monster that bites at 3,000 PSI and nobody was crawling in after me.

I stayed still, just watching that tail float a couple of inches from my face, mind racing with one question: *can he turn around?*

And right then, my brain jumped back to something I hadn't thought about in years.

I was five years old, back in West Monroe, Louisiana. We were at a swimming pool. I was in the shallow end, splashing around. My mom was helping my sister learn to swim, she was just a year older than me. I got out of the pool and walked around to the deep end. Nobody was looking. And I jumped in.

And just like that, I was under.

I remembered the fight. Arms flailing, lungs burning, everything getting dark. I was going down. I remembered thinking, clear as day, *I'm gonna die.* At five years old, I knew it.

Then a hand grabbed me.

Big, strong hand on my left arm, yanked me straight up out of the water. It was my dad. He'd been getting dressed, about to take us all to dinner. Just happened to step out and saw me go under.

He saved me. No question.

And now there I was, decades later, belly-down in a culvert, staring at an alligator's tail and thinking the same thing: *If this goes bad, no one's coming this time.* No hand. No rescue. Just me, a trash can, and fifty more yards of hope.

So I made a move.

I pushed the trash can forward, just enough to nudge his side.

That's when he exploded.

Water blasted into my face, slamming off the walls, the trash can, and my chest. That culvert turned into a thunder drum. He was hissing, tail thrashing, smashing into both sides like a wrecking ball.

I couldn't see much, but I could feel everything.

And what I felt… was relief.

He was still facing forward. He was too big to turn around.

That was the break I needed.

I planted my foot on a rock, wedged my shoulder behind the trash can, and started pushing.

He dug in, fighting with everything he had four legs braced in the slime, tail hammering behind him. He wanted to stay right where he was, in the dark, in control.

But I had no choice. I pushed again. Water slapped against my mouth. I turned my head just to breathe. My hands slid in algae. My knees got chewed up on busted-up concrete and hurricane rock.

And still, I pushed.

Every few feet, he threw another tantrum. Slammed his body into the culvert wall. Water rose over my chin again. I stopped. Let him wear himself out.

Then I pushed more.

I didn't know how long it had been. Time didn't exist down there, just breathing, moving, not dying.

Then I saw it.

Light.

Just a faint gray glow, far ahead. The manhole. The exit. The only way out.

And I thought—I just had to get him there.

That light got bigger. And the tail slams got stronger.

But I'd come too far.

We were almost there, me and him, and I could see the ropes hanging down now. Two of them dropped in from the manhole above. Big loops at the end. Lasso ropes, like we used for cattle.

That was the plan: I'd push the gator right into them, the game warden would grab the head, Sal would grab the tail, and we'd be done.

I yelled up, "Do not miss him! If he turns around in this space, I've got no room to fight!"

I gave one last shove.

The trash can tipped, bounced, and that alligator started to break through into the open end of the culvert.

Then I saw it.

One of the ropes fell.

Just slipped, like it was never tied off right. Dropped into the water and disappeared.

And I stopped breathing.

Because if they didn't catch him, if he made it past those ropes and turned around in that square opening, then I was about to go face-to-face with a pissed-off 350-pound gator in a concrete tunnel the width of my shoulders.

I froze.

I couldn't back up. I couldn't go forward. I was stuck between a monster and the last few feet of freedom and they'd dropped the rope.

Just let it fall.

Now there was nothing between me and that alligator but a prayer and a plastic trash can.

And I waited.

I didn't move. I didn't breathe too loud. I just lay there, flat on my belly, soaked, beat up, water lapping at my chin, waiting for them to fish the rope back up.

Seconds stretched. Every sound echoed. That gator still twitched in front of me, and the square opening where he could turn around was just a few feet away.

Then, finally, I heard it.

Zip.

That rope slid tight around his snout. Clean. Solid.

Then came the second rope, tail rope, Sal had it.

They had him.

Water exploded again as they hoisted him up, fighting all the way.

He was halfway out. Kicking, snapping, hissing. Three-quarters, then boom, he slipped and dropped right back into the water.

Huge splash. The culvert shook.

I braced myself. The trash can jolted. But then, another rope dropped in, quick. Clean. Looped the tail.

They pulled again.

This time, it held.

They got him up and over. Nine feet seven inches of raw, ancient power, dripping mud and hate.

Then it was my time to crawl out and crawl out I did.

Soaked, bleeding, exhausted and alive.

Chapter 2
Bayou Beginnings

Folks see what I do now—wrestling gators, building a sanctuary, handling calls no one else wants—and they think I must've always been built for this. The truth is, it started a long time ago, way before Gator Country, out in the bayous and backroads of Texas and Louisiana. I didn't grow up with money or peace. All I had was heat, humidity, and a whole lot of hard-won lessons. My parents fought nonstop, and when they finally broke up, I was on my own. I was 14, penniless, and pretty much alone. That was when the real learning began.

But before that, we traveled a lot.

I was born in Liberty County, Texas, in 1968. Nothing fancy—just the typical small-town beginnings. But I had terrible allergies. Terrible. The sort of allergies that clogged your head up with pressure and made it difficult to breathe in the heavy, humid Southeast Texas weather. The doctors told us that a drier climate might be better for me, and my dad—who was a Texas Highway Patrolman then—requested a transfer.

We landed in Amarillo. And it worked. The air was cleaner, drier. I could finally breathe.

But my mom didn't last long there.

She got homesick. Her family was from West Monroe, Louisiana, and after about a year of being in the Texas Panhandle, she was ready to go home. My dad made a tough choice—he gave up his patrolman job and moved the family to Louisiana. He became a local police officer there. My mom started working at a bakery.

It wasn't a bad start. Not yet.

For a little while, we had what you might call a normal family. I had an older sister, Stacy, and a younger sister, Holly. We had a roof, we had food, and I had both parents at home. But under the surface, things weren't right. The fights started small. Then they got worse. And by the time I was seven, the yelling, the tension—it never stopped.

From there, things only went downhill.

By the time I was seven, the fighting between my mom and dad was constant. Loud, angry, unpredictable. It could start over anything—money, chores, who said what—and it always ended the same way: broken dishes, screaming, and my sisters and I huddled in a bedroom, just waiting for it to be over.

Most kids want to have friends over. Sleepovers. Birthday parties. Not us. There was no way we could. You never knew when the next explosion was coming. One second, everything might seem calm, and the next, Kool-Aid's flying across the kitchen wall. Dishes breaking. Doors slamming. Fist-pounding kind of arguments.

We didn't really know what divorce meant, but we found ourselves wishing for it. Not because we didn't love our parents, but because we just wanted the noise to stop.

Sunday mornings were the worst. My dad wanted us to go to a strict church—real strict, the kind with rules for everything. My mom didn't want anything to do with it. Every week, like clockwork, there was a blow-up. 7:30 AM sharp, and we knew it was coming. Yelling about religion. About control. About everything.

That stuck with me.

All that fighting over faith left a bitter taste in my mouth when it came to religion.

It was like walking through a war zone, only the battlefield was our living room.

The worst part was the uncertainty. Never knowing when the next fight would begin, or how worse it would be. There were times we'd sit in silence, holding our breaths, hoping we wouldn't trigger either of them.

That went on for years. From the time I was seven until I was thirteen.

And then finally… they split.

But the chaos didn't end there.

When the divorce finally happened, I thought things might calm down. But they didn't. The yelling stopped, sure—but now came a new kind of hard.

My dad stayed in the main house. My mom moved out. I stayed with my dad. My sisters went with her.

They were still trying to figure out who got what—money, furniture, custody. One day, Mom came over, and it blew up again. They started fighting right there in the living room. Pushing. Yelling. Wrestling on the floor. I didn't know who started it, but I knew I had to do something.

I called 911.

A female officer showed up—West Monroe PD. And my mom even fought with her. I'll never forget it. No kid should ever have to watch their parents go at it like that.

Eventually, the divorce was finalized. But what came after hit even harder.

Before the divorce, life was at least stable. We had food. A roof. I could go see a movie or buy school clothes. After the split, I moved into a little one-room apartment with my dad. He was a Louisiana police officer. And if you don't know, those guys don't make much money.

That's when I met poverty for the first time.

No food in the fridge. No money for anything extra. I was fourteen years old and suddenly on my own more than I ever thought possible.

Those years between fourteen and seventeen—those are the years a kid needs support the most. Love, guidance, structure. I didn't have any of it. My dad was doing the best he could, but the truth was, I was basically raising myself.

And that's when I started learning how to survive.

I didn't have a choice. At fourteen, I had to figure out how to take care of myself.

My dad managed to get me two Montgomery leg-hold traps. That was the start.

Every morning before school, I'd wake up at 4:00 AM, walk two or three miles to the creeks and rivers, and check those traps. I was catching raccoons, possums, even a beaver or two—whatever I could sell for fur money. Some weeks, I'd make enough to buy another trap or two. Eventually, I had about two dozen going at once. I was making maybe forty, forty-five dollars a week. That was a lot to me back then.

Still, it was hard work. Dirty. Cold. Wet. And I started thinking—there's gotta be a better way.

So I bought a lawnmower.

That trap money got me a small push mower, and I started knocking on doors in the neighborhood. Ten bucks a yard. Just me, mowing grass, trying to survive. The work came fast. I did one yard, then two, then ten. Before long, I had myself a full-blown little mowing business.

That's when I first understood capitalism. You work hard, treat people fairly, and they'll call you back. I was fifteen, running a lawn crew of one.

But I still felt like I didn't belong. I'd go to school and see other kids in polo shirts and penny loafers—smelling like cologne, not chain grease. They weren't working before class. They weren't walking trap lines or mowing yards until dark. Their money came from their parents. Mine came from sweat.

Still, I wanted to look like I belonged too. So I saved up, went to Dillard's, and spent $37 on a red, blue, and white striped polo shirt. Wore it every other day. Didn't care what anyone thought. That was my proof—I could play the part too.

Then I got a second job. I started scooping ice cream at Baskin-Robbins. My schedule was simple: school during the day, lawn work in the afternoon, ice cream at night. I was doing whatever it took.

That's how I got by.

But life wasn't done testing me yet.

By the time I was sixteen, I was holding it together. I had a routine. I had work. I had a little dignity. Then my dad came in and said he was leaving.

We were already living outside Hainesville, Louisiana. And when I say "outside," I mean it. Eleven, maybe twelve miles from the nearest town. No neighbors. No traffic. Just woods and long stretches of road. Quiet enough to hear crickets argue. That kind of rural.

I didn't argue. We had already packed up and moved once. I'd started over again.

School was different, but I did what I always did—I worked, I played ball, I kept my head down. And I was good at baseball. Real good. That summer, I made the All-Stars. Got a pre-letter from a Louisiana college that had their eye on me for a scholarship.

Then, just as the season was peaking, Dad sat me down and said, "I'm leaving."

Just like that.

He told me he was packing up and heading to Texas. Said I could come if I wanted, but he was going either way.

I told him I had to stay—I couldn't walk away from the team, not in the middle of All-Stars. I had one shot at a scholarship, one shot at something bigger than working myself into the ground every day. He said, "You do what you need to do." And then he left.

I came home the next day and found an empty house. No furniture. No food. No note. Just silence. I picked up the phone to call a friend, and the line was dead.

No dial tone.

He'd cut the service.

So I grabbed my bag and started walking. Eleven miles back to the city. Got there around ten at night, knocked on a teammate's door, and asked if I could crash for the night. He said sure—but beyond that, no promises.

The next day at practice, I told my coach. He listened. Said they'd try to help me find a place to stay—if I was serious about finishing the season. I was. But I was also hungry.

No food. No home. Nothing but a bag of clothes and whatever was left of my pride.

That afternoon, I walked into town and found a restaurant where my dad used to know a guy. I walked in, told the man I'd do anything—wash dishes, sweep, haul trash—whatever it took. I just needed a meal.

He looked me up and down and said, "I don't have room on the payroll. But if you'll wash dishes, you can eat off what comes back."

So that's what I did. Picked the cleanest plates off the tray, ate what was left, and kept washing.

After the season ended and my coach had to move out of state, I ran out of options. I didn't have a roof, I didn't have a job, and I didn't have anyone left to ask.

That's when I realized I had to make the hardest call of my life.

I picked up the phone and dialed my mother's number. We hadn't spoken much in the last couple of years. I'd been living with my dad, and there was bad blood between them, and some between her and me, too. Still, I swallowed my pride and dialed.

When she picked up, I said, "Mother, I've got a problem. I don't have anywhere to go."

She paused.

Then she asked the obvious. "Where's your dad?"

I said, "I don't know. He's gone."

After some back-and-forth, she finally said, "You can come back. You can finish your senior year here."

So I packed my stuff and caught a ride back to West Monroe. More specifically, I landed just across the bridge in Ouachita Parish.

We moved into a small, two-bedroom apartment—my mom, my older sister, my younger sister, and I. It was crowded. Tense. But I had a spot. A bed. A shot at finishing school.

I picked up where I left off at Baskin-Robbins, scooping ice cream after school. I kept my grades up. I got through it.

But right near graduation, the pressure in that little apartment hit a breaking point.

I walked home on my last day of high school and found everything I owned in three bags on the front porch.

My mother met me at the door and said, "My job is done. It's time for you to go."

Just like that.

So I called a friend—someone I'd known through that final year of high school—and asked if he had any ideas. His grandmother had an old, busted-up single-wide trailer she was willing to rent for $300 a month. That was all I had, so I jumped on it.

The floor had holes. The walls were thin. But I had a room. I had a closet. I had a little freedom.

Four days after graduation, I picked up another job driving a dump truck, hauling away construction debris. Worked that from 6 AM to 2 PM, then headed to Baskin-Robbins from 3 to 11.

Day after day, shift after shift, I kept grinding. I didn't have a plan yet, but I kept going.

Because deep down, I already knew what life had been teaching me for years:

No one was coming to save me.

If I wanted to move forward, I'd have to dig my way out.

Chapter 3
Weight of Hardship

I met Samantha three weeks after moving back to West Monroe. I was eighteen. She was seventeen, still a junior in high school. Brown hair, deep brown eyes, pretty smile—she was easy to notice. We started dating, and before long, we were serious.

We stayed together my entire senior year. She was the one thing I looked forward to, the only good distraction from working, scraping by, and figuring out life on my own. I was running a dump truck by day, scooping ice cream by night, and coming home to a trailer that wasn't worth the ground it sat on. Raccoons crawled through a hole in the floor, climbed on my bed, and stared at me like they paid rent.

My roommate Ty didn't live that way—not in his mind, anyway. He worked a part-time job, came home early, and threw parties. That trailer was full of people most nights. High schoolers, college kids, music loud enough to shake the walls. I'd drag in from Baskin Robbins at eleven and find my own house packed with strangers.

I didn't have time for that sort of life. I worked two jobs to merely have food in my mouth and pay the rent. Samantha was my respite, my sane. I didn't know what happened next, but I knew I didn't want to lose her. I just kept on working, hoping, waiting for us to work out the future.

It was somewhere in the midst of all that that I encountered Homer Farrington.

Homer and his family visited Baskin Robbins every Sunday after church—him, his wife, and two little children. Same time each week, about 1:30. I had their orders memorized: the children had chocolate chip, his wife asked for mint chocolate chip, and Homer always had pralines and cream.

It began innocently, mere small talk. But as time passed, Homer became genuinely interested in me. He asked questions—where I was from, what I was striving for, what I wanted to do in life. I didn't have many answers, but I had integrity. He appreciated that. Soon, he was having me over for supper.

It was the first honest-to-goodness family table I'd eaten at in a long time. They treated me with kindness, like I was important. Homer realized that I didn't have an effective means of transportation to get to work, so after dinner one night, he stated, "Let me get you a vehicle."

I didn't know how to respond to that. I'd had people be nice before, but nobody ever stuck their neck out for me like that.

Sure enough, he cosigned a loan for me to purchase a bit used Mazda B2200 pickup—two-tone blue, light and dark. It was $3,800, which seemed like a lot of money to me. I had payments: $189 a month. That was big-time money, but it was all mine. It took me to work, and it made me feel like I was getting my life together at last.

Homer also gave me something else, something small but significant. He gave me a pair of lizard skin boots. They weren't brand new, but they were sharp, and they felt like the best thing I had. I didn't have much, but I had those boots.

That meant something to me—like I wasn't just the poor kid in the broken-down trailer anymore. I had my own truck. I had my boots. I was getting it done.

And then one evening, I came home, and the boots were gone.

I didn't have a lot of things that I felt were mine, so when those boots went missing, it hit harder than it should've. I got off my shift at Baskin Robbins, went to my room, and the one decent possession I had—the lizard skin boots Homer gave me—were gone.

I knew what happened. Ty had people over. Another party, another mess. That trailer was never really my space. It was just a roof with bad company.

The next morning, driving the dump truck down Louisville Avenue, I passed the Armed Forces recruiting office. Every branch was in there—Marines, Navy, Army, Air Force, Coast Guard. I didn't have to think hard. I pulled the truck in and parked.

I started with the Marines. They came at me strong, heavy on the pride, the few and the proud. I talked for a bit, but their pitch was too much. Next was the Navy, but I didn't like the idea of being stuck on a ship for months at a time.

Then the Army. They had a sales angle too, promising police work, even working with dogs. That sounded good—I always loved animals. They gave me paperwork, and it sounds like a solid path.

But before I left, I stopped in the Air Force office. No sales pitch there. Just a recruiter who looked me up and down and said, "Can you even make the grades to get in?"

That hit different. I wasn't a great student. C's were a win for me in high school. But I wasn't about to let someone tell me I wasn't good enough without trying.

I asked what I needed to qualify. The recruiter said I had to score an 81 on the ASVAB test. Two weeks later, I took it and pulled an 84.

That was it. I signed up for the United States Air Force.

So I told Samantha—we're doing this. I'm signing with the United States Air Force. March of 1988—that was my date. I was proud of myself. I'd made it in, and I finally felt like I had a future to chase.

And it wasn't just me. In my mind, it was us. We were going forward together.

We both knew the truth, though—she came from money, and I came from nothing. Her family wasn't always wealthy, but that changed after a tragic accident. One night, they were driving when a horse ran loose onto the highway. They hit it head-on. The landowner was held responsible for letting the animal get out, and the family won a significant settlement. That money changed their life—they moved up, lived comfortably, didn't want for anything.

I, on the other hand, was living in a busted trailer with raccoons crawling through the floor, driving a dump truck by day, scooping ice cream by night, and still barely scraping by.

That gap between us was obvious. The military felt like my only real shot at closing it. I couldn't give her the life she was used to—not the way I was going. The Air Force was my ticket to something better.

The military felt like my only real shot at changing that. I couldn't offer her the life her family had given her—not the way I was going. The Air Force was my ticket to something better. I had my date to leave: March 1988.

For the first time, it felt like I had a real future lined up— and for once, I wasn't just surviving.

I shipped off to basic training, thinking I had everything to fight for. Boot camp was tough, but I kept my head down and pushed through, always telling myself that I wasn't doing this alone—that Samantha and I had a plan.

After basic training, I went straight into technical school. That's when the phone calls started getting fewer. Then they stopped altogether. No letters. No messages. Silence.

I knew something was wrong, but I told myself she was just busy. I kept dialing anyway. Then one day, the letter showed up—the Dear John. She'd made up her mind. I was on my own now.

That was a different kind of hit. When you're that far from home, living in a bunk with strangers, and the one person you thought would be waiting for you just cuts the line—it hits you deeper than the yelling drill sergeants ever could.

When I finally graduated from training, I went back to West Monroe for a visit. I couldn't let it end on paper. I wanted to look her in the eye.

I showed up in my dress blues, shined up and squared away, and knocked on her door. Her mother answered—guarded, defensive. I asked for thirty seconds, just to say goodbye. She agreed.

Samantha came to the door. I asked her why. Why no calls, no answers—what happened?

All she said was, "You did what you wanted to do. Now it's time for you to go be you."

That was it. She shut the door. I turned, got in my little blue truck, and didn't look back.

Chapter 4
Across the Wire

I couldn't keep the door open on my feelings for Samantha, even if I wanted to. My military leave was running out, and it was time to get my head right. The best way I knew how: reconnect with old high school friends and blow off some steam. I had three weeks to harden up before reporting to airbase ground defense at Fort Dix, New Jersey. The next phase wasn't about feelings—it was foxholes, live rounds, and learning how to survive when everything's aimed to kill.

Fort Dix, New Jersey, wasn't what I imagined. I'd joined the Air Force, but this was Army-run, no question about it. They didn't care what patch was on your shoulder—we were all just bodies in boots, headed for the dirt.

Six weeks of field training, tents, and foxholes. No beds, no barracks—just ground. August in New Jersey isn't kind either. It was humid, hot, and miserable. The only break from the heat was when it stormed, and then you just got wet and miserable.

They taught us how to defend a base like our lives depended on it—because in wartime, it does. We dug in, ran drills, learned the terrain, and slept wherever we fell. You got comfortable being uncomfortable.

We all knew the last night was coming—the final test. They didn't hide it. They told us we'd hit a live-fire exercise and we'd either prove we were ready, or we weren't.

They moved us out to a big hill around six in the evening. We sat there until dark, weapons loaded, gear checked, waiting for the sky to fall. As soon as the sun dropped, they lit up the sky with illumination rounds—bright enough to see every shadow moving in the distance.

Then the machine guns opened up. Real guns, real rounds, ripping from the top of the opposite hill. You could see the tracers flying ten, maybe twelve feet overhead. No sound like it—loud, sharp, and way too close.

Four of us got pulled back—me included. I felt a hand grab my ankle and drag me out of line. They put a military policewoman in front of me and said, "She doesn't make it, you don't graduate."

That was it. No further explanation. She was my responsibility, and failure wasn't an option. I tapped her leg and said, "We're finishing this. Period."

And then we went down that hill, into the dark, into the noise, and into hell.

We crawled low, the dirt wet and heavy, our elbows and knees grinding into rocks and roots. Every few yards, a grenade simulator would blast, throwing fire and sound through the night. The ground shook, and the air reeked of smoke and spent powder.

She flinched at every blast, but I stayed close, tapping her leg, whispering, "Keep moving. Don't stop." The rule was simple: stop moving, you're a target.

Halfway down, a simulator blew right next to her, flipped her over on her back. She gasped, wheezing, eyes wide like she'd just been sucker punched. I flipped her back, got her on her elbows.

"We're not stopping," I told her. "Breathe later—move now."

She nodded, barely, and kept crawling.

By the time we hit the low ground, the machine guns sounded like they were inside our skulls. Tracers burned across the sky, some close enough to feel the heat. We snaked through concertina wire, craters, and barricades, my job to keep her moving and keep us both alive.

Finally, we got to the last set of obstacles—deep pits lined with stone and wire, each one hiding another blast if you got too close. We crawled around them, tossed our training grenades into the designated nests, and pressed forward. No thinking, just moving.

Forty-five minutes later, we crawled past the final marker. The whistle blew, signaling the end.

We made it.

I helped her up, both of us covered in mud, smoke, and sweat. She didn't say much—she didn't have to. We'd finished it. That was enough.

The next morning, they handed out our next assignments. I was ready to leave New Jersey and find out what the Air Force had planned for me next.

They lined us up outside the chow hall after breakfast, all of us filthy, sore, and half-wrecked from the night before. One by one, they started calling names, handing out sealed envelopes— our new orders.

Everybody was excited. Guys were getting stationed all over—Florida, California, big-name bases you'd actually heard of. I was near the end of the list, waiting it out, already guessing I'd get stuck somewhere random. But I still held onto that recruiter's promise: I'd stay stateside. That's what they told me.

Finally, they called my name. I stepped up, took the envelope, and ripped it open right there on the gravel.

I didn't even recognize the word on the page. Zweibrücken, Germany.

I read it twice, like that would make it say something else. But there it was—Zweibrücken. I had no clue where it was, no clue how to say it, and definitely no clue how far from home that was.

So much for stateside.

I shook my head, stuffed the paper in my pocket, and started packing my gear. The next day, I was in a cab headed from Fort Dix to JFK airport, New York City. I'd never been anywhere like that in my life.

We flew out of JFK on a giant two-decker plane—the biggest thing I'd ever seen. Felt like a flying skyscraper. Nine hours later, we landed in England to refuel, then another hop to Frankfurt, Germany.

Instructions said someone from Zweibrücken Air Base would pick me up. So I waited. And wait was all I did.

For four hours. Then six. Then eight. I bid goodbye to the fellows who accompanied me on my flight when they got scooped up by their units, got into their vans, and went off to their sanctuaries. By 9:30 that night, everyone was gone. The place was empty, now, me being accompanied by just my duffel and dead silence.

With no contact number and no sign of military personnel at the airport, I could only rely on my own. So I flagged a cab and asked how much it'd cost to get to Zweibrücken. The driver did the math—about $250 in today's money. I didn't see another option.

Three hours later, we pulled up to the gate. The military police looked half-surprised, half-confused. Someone finally admitted they'd forgotten to send a ride. Great start.

But I was there, tired, broke, but finally there. The security forces scooped me up, took me to the dorms, and before I even had time to unpack, they handed me a German beer and said, "Welcome to Europe."

We drank late into the night. I didn't even know what I was drinking—it was cold and strong, that's all I cared about. I woke up the next morning on the 50-yard line of the base football field. I wasn't alone—some girl was next to me, no clue who she was, never did figure it out. That was Europe.

Life on base settled into a rhythm—guard shifts, patrols, and long nights trying to stay awake in freezing cold towers. It was a recon base, just a few miles from the French border, small and quiet most days. But NATO exercises changed all that.

One exercise put me in charge of a fire team defending the west side of the base. We took up position under an old World War II tank—cold steel, barely a foot and a half off the ground. Cramped, but solid cover. Night vision scopes up, weapons hot, eyes on the treeline.

Then they came—three, maybe four hundred "enemy" troops flooding through the woods. We lit them up. M60 machine guns, M203 grenade launchers—everything we had. Blank rounds cracking like real ones, lasers slicing through the dark, the noise bouncing off steel and dirt. We were locked in, holding the line.

Then—out of nowhere—a grenade rolled in from behind us. Behind us. That wasn't possible. The enemy was supposed to be in front, nowhere near our rear flank.

I turned just in time to catch a pair of legs disappearing into the night. One of the NATO "bad guys," meant to simulate the enemy, had circled behind us and tossed a grenade under the tank to "spice things up." Nobody told us. Nobody cleared it.

I shouted for my guys to roll out, but it was too late. The grenade popped—smoke, heat, ears ringing. The tank acted like an echo chamber, amplifying everything. My guys were coughing, blind through gas masks, screaming from the shock and the noise with no hearing protection.

I pulled them out, one by one, then went hunting. I found the guy—a staff sergeant—standing there proud of himself like he'd just made the simulation "real." I lost it. I grabbed him, slammed him down in the dirt, and beat the hell out of him right there in front of God and everybody.

The exercise horn sounded—pause everything. The MPs came running. I expected trouble, but my team backed me up. They told the truth. That staff sergeant? He was discharged two weeks later.

That was just Europe—good times, bad decisions, and doing what you had to do to get by. A few weeks later, my orders came in. The Berlin Wall was falling, the world was changing, and the Air Force was cutting people early.

I signed the papers and got out early. Time to head home— and start the next chapter.

About three weeks after that fight under the tank, word came down: the Berlin Wall had fallen.

I never thought I'd witness something that historic, but there I was—boots on the ground in Berlin. The wall was coming down in chunks, section by section. East Germans stood frozen on the other side, still not believing they could cross. Russian soldiers stood by, weapons in hand, but didn't move.

Then one East German made a run for it—just took off and bolted through. No shots fired. And when that first guy made it, the dam broke. A flood of people from the East poured through, hugging strangers, crying, touching everything like it might vanish.

I broke a piece of the wall off myself—kept it. A jagged little reminder that sometimes the world actually does change overnight.

A week later, they announced the early outs. With the Cold War cooling off, they didn't need as many boots in Europe.

I'd done my time, seen things I never imagined, made mistakes, and made memories. But it was time for a new chapter.

I signed out of Germany, packed my things, and caught a flight back to Louisiana. The plan was clear: I was headed home to start police academy. A new uniform, a new mission—but this time, I'd be standing guard in my own backyard.

And that's when the next chapter of my life began.

Chapter 5
From Airman to Spy

I signed out of Frankfurt, Germany, boots still dirty from the motor pool, and caught a military hop back to the States. First stop: Fort Dix, New Jersey. That's where they processed my paperwork, asked me all the questions, handed me a DD-214, and told me I was free to go. Just like that. One day I'm an airman, the next day I'm a civilian with a duffel bag and some free time at hand before starting my next career.

From there, I boarded a flight to Shreveport, Louisiana. The heat hit me like a wet towel fresh from the dryer. As promised, my dad met me, waiting at the curb.

We drove west through pine trees and pastureland, crossing the state line into East Texas. Neither of us spoke for a while.

Somewhere past Marshall, maybe close to Longview, my dad finally asked, "So what now?"

"I'm thinking about joining the police academy."

He nodded, one hand on the wheel. "You'd be good at it."

He wasn't the advice-giving type, so his approval meant something. I didn't know a damn thing about being a cop, but I knew how to follow orders and show up on time. That's pretty much what got me through the early days. A couple of weeks later, I was signed up for the academy.

I had a little space between signing and starting, so I made good use of it. Hit a few parties, caught up with old faces, stayed out too late. It wasn't a wild run, just a way to blow the carbon out before putting the uniform back on—different uniform, same weight.

The academy was in Nacogdoches, Texas. Hot and humid. I wasn't the smartest in the room—a C-average learner most of my life—but I paid attention, kept my mouth shut, and pushed through. I'd done harder things. The days were long and full of stuff meant to break you down and build you into someone who could hold the line.

I passed everything. Nothing flashy, nothing pretty. Just steady. When they handed me the badge, I didn't feel proud so much as clear-headed. I wasn't naive. I'd been in military already. I knew this wasn't hero work—it was grind, risk, and showing up when most people wouldn't.

I was in. And it wouldn't be long before the real test showed up in a place I never expected—high school.

A couple of weeks after graduation, I got a call. Not from anyone I knew. The guy on the other end didn't give his name— just said he was with the department and wanted to know if I'd be willing to talk about "a different kind of assignment."

He gave me directions and said, "Meet us behind the McDonald's. We'll be in a silver Dodge Durango."

That was it.

I figured either I was being recruited for something special, or I was about to get kidnapped. Either way, I showed up.

Sure enough, there they were—two plainclothes guys in a parked Durango, windows cracked like they were waiting on a drug deal. I got in the back seat. One of them passed me a manila folder without looking up from his fries.

"We're looking for someone who can pass for a high school student," he said.

I paused. "To talk to them, or…?"

"No," he said. "To be one."

I sat back, trying not to laugh. "You're serious?"

They were. This wasn't patrol. No badge. No radio. No cruiser. They wanted me to enroll at an actual high school under a fake name, go to class, eat the square pizza, and quietly figure out who was dealing drugs.

Apparently, I looked the part. I was young enough, hadn't made waves in the department, and could blend in. Or disappear, depending on how you looked at it. I guess being average-looking and a C-student finally paid off.

I nodded like I understood what I was getting into, but I didn't. I'd barely made it through school the first time. The idea of sneaking through it again—while pretending to be someone else—sounded crazy.

So I called my dad.

I laid it out—Durango, fake ID, cafeteria recon, the whole deal.

He didn't even hesitate. "Sounds like a good way to get shot or flunk out."

Fair enough.

"Why not just be a cop the normal way?" he asked.

I didn't have a great answer. But I couldn't let it go. Maybe it was the challenge. Maybe it was the chaos. Maybe I just liked the idea of doing something most people wouldn't.

And to me, it felt simple: better a bird in the hand than one in the bush. I had a job offer, and that was more than most rookies could say.

So the next day, I called the commander of the narcotics task force and accepted the job. He asked when I could start.

I told him, "Give me three days."

I packed everything I owned, hitched up a trailer, and moved two hours south, from East Texas to Southeast Texas. Found a small apartment. Unloaded. Got settled.

And just like that, I was back in school.

Only this time, I wasn't there to graduate.

I hadn't officially said yes to the job yet when I saw Tiffany for the first time.

I'd stopped at a roadside restaurant outside of Beaumont, still thinking over the offer to go undercover. The hostess sat me at a table for two. I was alone.

Then the waitress walked up—dark hair, soft Cajun accent, name tag said Tiffany.

"Long day?" she asked, handing me a menu.

"Yeah," I said. "Something like that."

She brought my food, checked in now and then—nothing flashy, just kind and confident. When the check came, I saw a smiley face and a phone number written at the bottom.

I didn't know it then, but that small move would change everything. Tiffany would end up becoming my first wife.

The first few weeks felt like punishment. Not because of the danger, but because of the routine. Eight to three. Bells ringing. Classrooms with squeaky chairs. I was sitting through algebra again like it was Groundhog Day, only this time I wasn't just trying to pass—I was trying to fit in.

This little town—Vidor, Texas—was tight-knit and cliquish. Outsiders didn't just walk in and get welcomed. You had to earn your place. That meant going to football games, hanging out at lunch, and asking about people's cousins. It wasn't just undercover work—it was full-blown high school immersion.

The students were skeptical at first. I was new, quiet, and didn't have a backstory anyone could verify. But slowly, I started to break in. It took months. Months of cafeteria food, forced pep rallies, and pretending I didn't already know how the mitochondria worked.

Eventually, they got comfortable. I stopped being the new guy and started being just another guy. That's when the real work could begin.

Once I had their trust, I could change things up. I'd start showing up late. Skipping classes. Getting written up. The principal didn't know who I was—nobody in that building did—so I could get in trouble without blowing my cover.

And that was the goal: get expelled.

Once I was officially booted from school, I could still hang around. Recess, after school, strip malls—wherever they were, I could be. And believe me, I'd always been good at recess. Even in elementary school, that was my strongest subject.

That freedom changed everything. I didn't have to sit through full days anymore. I was showing up just to maintain connections, and cases started rolling in. One by one, people started talking. Small deals at first. Then the bigger ones. I had built trust, and now it was paying off.

By the time it was done, I'd made more narcotics cases as a high school student than any other undercover agent in Texas history. That wasn't bragging. That was just a fact.

Things were going well—almost too well. And when that happens, you start looking over your shoulder.

Because success like that never comes without a price.

About five months in, I got a call from the Narcotics Task Force asking me to come into the office. That alone was odd—I never went in. My job happened in hallways, bathrooms, cars, and backyards. I didn't have a desk.

When I walked in, it wasn't just my commander. The chief of police and the assistant district attorney were also sitting there. No one smiled.

The chief started it off:

"You remember the guy from your last case?"

"Yeah," I said.

"That name ring any bells?"

"No, sir. Not from around here."

He nodded toward the ADA.

"That's his son."

Everything stopped.

Turned out I'd just made a textbook case on the assistant DA's kid—ecstasy distribution, solid evidence. Normally, they'd be readying charges. But this wasn't normal anymore. I wasn't just an undercover now—I was a problem.

They didn't directly ask me to back off. But the message was clear: let this one go.

Under Texas law, the officer who makes the arrest has final say on whether charges proceed. That meant they couldn't force my hand. But everyone in that room expected me to fold. They gave me three days' leave—"with pay"—to think about it.

I went home and talked to my dad, who had three decades in law enforcement. I talked to Tiffany. Neither one tried to steer me. Just: "It's your call. But whatever you decide—you'll have to live with it."

I thought about the other kids I'd booked. They didn't get second chances. Same drugs, same charges. Only difference? Their parents didn't work in the courthouse.

Three days later, I walked back in.

The commander asked, "Well?"

I said, "I took this job to treat everyone the same. I'm not dropping it."

Then I slid my badge across the table and walked out.

I didn't know what would come next. But I knew what couldn't continue: selective justice.

Undercover work gave me everything and took just as much. It's how I met Tiffany, the woman I'd marry—and how I'd eventually lose her. The job let me into worlds most cops never see, earned me recognition I never asked for, and buried me under pressure I couldn't explain. By the time it was over, I'd be promoted, broken, and alone.

A few days after I resigned from Vidor PD, Tiffany and I were sitting on a beach, just trying to decompress. Out of the blue, she asked, "What do you really want to do now?" I told her the same thing I'd always wanted—to be a patrolman. Not narcotics. Not undercover. Just a basic patrol cop.

She nodded and said, "Well, my grandfather's the justice of the peace over in Chambers County. He knows the sheriff pretty well. Maybe I can get you an interview."

A few days later, her grandfather called and said, "I've got your application here at the office—come fill it out." So I did. And while I'm sitting there filling it out, the sheriff himself walks in. Turns out, he knew my dad from back when he worked there. We started talking about my dad for a bit, and then he asked what position I was applying for.

I told him, "Law enforcement. Hoping for patrol."

He looked at me and said, "Well, I've got an opening on the narcotics task force. You give me a year to eighteen months on that, and I'll pull you out and put you on patrol."

Here we go again.

A few days later, I took the job. This time, it was deep undercover—Galveston Bay, shrimp boats, oyster boats. That whole scene was rough. A lot of illegal activity, a lot of transients, and a constant stream of drugs coming in from offshore oil rigs. My job was to blend in and figure out who was moving what.

Chambers County was like most small towns—cliquish and hard to break into. I spent a lot of time at local bars, worked a shrimp boat job for a few days, and slowly started earning enough trust to get inside. These weren't small-time kids like before. These were grown men with records, nothing to lose, and bad tempers.

All the while, Tiff and I kept building our relationship. About five or six months in, we got engaged. I was waist-deep in the narcotics world, but still trying to plan a future with her at the same time.

One of the most dangerous nights I had working near Galveston Bay started like any other: quiet, grimy, and heavy with anticipation. We'd been working the shrimp boats long enough to figure out who was moving the product in from offshore oil rigs, and now it was time to make the buy. I had six thousand dollars in my coat pocket—marked bills from the task force—and a knot in my stomach that hadn't left me all week.

I walked into a seedy dockside bar where the meeting was supposed to happen. It was dark, the air thick with cigarette smoke and beer sweat. I'd put in enough time there—drinking just enough, listening more than I talked, making friends with the bartender—that most of the regulars didn't give me a second look anymore.

One of the shrimp boat guys I'd seen around motioned toward the back. "We're doing this in the bathroom."

It was February, cold enough for my jacket to make sense, which helped conceal the little .380 I had tucked into the small of my back. No one on the ground had my six. No car parked out front with another officer. Just me, a wire taped to my chest, and a Customs helicopter in the sky that wouldn't be much help if things got tight in a tiled box with no windows.

I walked into the bathroom and saw three men. Right there by the sink sat two kilos of cocaine, still wrapped in duct tape. No small talk. One of them laid a stainless steel .357 Magnum on the counter like a dealer showing his cards. Another stared me down and asked, "You the police?"

That question hit harder than the cold tile under my boots.

I had a split second to decide what this was going to be. If I denied it and they didn't buy it, someone might go for that revolver. If I reached for my pistol, I had to hope I was faster than at least two of them. And if the wire picked up gunshots, maybe the helicopter would spot bodies on the ground later—but they wouldn't be able to stop it.

I stood there, heart pounding, and weighed it all. The backup wasn't close enough. The gun wasn't fast enough. The only thing I had going for me was the six thousand in my pocket.

So I pulled it out. Quiet. Calm. Counted on instinct and psychology. I laid the money on the counter next to the dope like it was just business, like none of this rattled me.

They didn't say anything for a moment. Then one of them reached under his coat, pulled out a crumpled grocery bag, shoved the coke inside, handed it to me, and scooped up the cash.

And just like that, it was over.

I walked out with two bricks of cocaine. They walked out with six grand.

Sometimes, when guns are on the counter and the walls are closing in, it's not your weapon or your wire that saves you—it's acting like the money does all the talking.

Chapter 6
The Breaking Point

Things had started to shift. I'd done the work heavy for close to a year—two departments, plenty of miles, plenty of close calls. Word started getting around. My face was too familiar in too many wrong places. Even the commander admitted it: I was going to get recognized eventually, and it wouldn't end clean.

So they pulled me off the front line. Said it was "for my safety," which was a polite way of saying the risk wasn't worth the headlines. I didn't argue.

Next thing I knew, I was a trainer.

The commander of the task force gave me the call himself.

"We got a new kid," he said. "Fresh out of the academy. He's 21. You're going to bring him up."

His name was Sonny. Good-looking kid—tall, clean cut, walked like someone who still believed in the rules. Black. That mattered, given what we were working.

We had divided zones—white town, Hispanic town, black town. Crack was surging hard in the black neighborhoods, so that's where they sent us. They gave Sonny a cherry red Camaro. No markings, fresh plates. My job was to ride with him, make sure he didn't get himself killed while he learned how to buy crack on the street.

I wasn't undercover anymore. Not technically. Now I was the guy who watched your back while you *were*.

Most days, I still dressed down—old jeans, faded t-shirts, just enough of a look to blend without being noticed. But there was a shift. I was no longer in it for the buy. I was there to keep the kid safe. Keep the deal alive. Make sure neither of us ended up bleeding out behind a trash bin.

That's what it had come to.

And that's how I met Sonny.

That night we were working a neighborhood out in the county—mostly Black, poor, real tight houses, no streetlights, just porch lights and whatever glowed off a TV inside. You could smell hot grease in the air, maybe barbecue, maybe trash. It was muggy, the kind of thick heat that made people come outside just to sit and breathe.

Sonny and I were in an old Z28—deep red, T-tops off, windows down, music up. Something bass-heavy, slow, with enough swing to sell the illusion. We were playing the part. He drove, I rode shotgun.

"Follow my lead," I told him. "Don't talk unless you have to. Just watch. Feel it."

He nodded once. No nerves showing, but I knew they were there.

We rolled into the neighborhood easy, not creeping, just slow enough to be noticed but not remembered. People on porches watched us roll by—some nodded, some didn't.

Then we saw her.

She was out front with a paper cup in her hand—vodka, probably. Mid-thirties, skinny, short hair, cutoff shorts, and a tank top. Didn't give us a signal or anything. Just looked us over once and kept sipping like we were nothing new.

That was the invitation. We accepted it.

We ease past and she calls out, "What y'all lookin' for?"

I said, "Rocks."

"How much?"

"Forty."

She nods. "A'ight, make the block and come back—I'll have it."

So we loop around—just a couple minutes—and sure enough, she's still there, but now she's got a little change in her tone. Says, "I can't get it here. Gotta take me down the road."

So I tell her, "Fine," and I hop in the backseat while she slides up front with Sonny. I always took the back when we had a rider—gives me a better angle to watch hands, pockets, movement. Let Sonny play the front like he's the guy with the money.

We start down the road, and I notice pretty quick—we're about to cross the line. See, there's this red light, and right past it is Harris County. We were working for Chambers County. Now, I'm not saying you can't make an arrest out of your jurisdiction, but doing it across county lines means you've got to deal with a whole different judge, a different jail, and in this case, Houston. That's the biggest county jail in Texas, and a paperwork nightmare.

We pull into this apartment complex. She hops out, says she'll be right back. Door shuts. We sit in silence. Engine idling. Sonny's gripping the wheel like he's trying to remember everything I told him.

So I tell Sonny, "When she gets back in the car, *do not* take the dope. Not until we're back in Chambers."

She climbs into the car, settles in like she's done this dance a hundred times, turns halfway toward Sonny, all flirty and casual, but her eyes—her eyes are working angles.

We roll down the street slow, just enough to not spook her. The complex fades behind us, and that damned red light looms ahead. The line between Chambers and Harris.

Of course, it's red.

We stop. No traffic, but we sit. Engine rumbling. I can see the commander's headlights in the mirror, two cars back, listening in through the wire.

Everyone's silent. Nobody breathing heavy. Just the low thump of bass from some house down the block and the wind brushing across the open roof.

Green.

Sonny eases through, keeps it smooth. Hits about 60.

And that's when she does it—just like nothing—leans over, reaches into that mystery purse of hers, pulls out a little twisted corner of baggie, and hands it to Sonny.

He takes it. Doesn't flinch.

She leans back with that same half-smile.

I reach forward from the back seat, calm and steady, and flip open my badge with my right hand. Hold it just enough in front of her face so there's no mistaking what it is.

"Chambers County Narcotics Task Force," I say. "You're under arrest."

Her smile vanishes like a light switched off.

As soon as I flashed the badge, it was like a bomb went off under her. She shot straight through the T-tops—half out the car, trying to escape. I reached up, grabbed her under the neck, just to keep her in the seat. She froze, wind whipping through her hair— and then her wig flew off. Gone. Looked like a damn beaver rolled down the street. She was bald. Shiny bald. And *pissed*.

I'm yelling at Sonny, "Pull over!" The radio's crackling—our boss behind us yelling the same thing. Chaos.

Then she bites me. Hard. Right on the arm. All the way through—felt like she hit bone. I ripped my arm back, blood coming through my sleeve.

We finally stopped the car. Officers pulled up. We grabbed her wig off the street. Boss looks at me, then her, and says, "We're taking her to jail."

They cuffed her and loaded her up. I'm standing there, bleeding, holding a chewed-up arm and a busted wig, wondering what the hell just happened.

And I'm not just bit—bitten. This wasn't some drunk slap or scratch. She locked onto my arm like a damn pit bull. And here's the kicker—we find out later she's a prostitute. Not just that—she's HIV positive. Full-blown AIDS.

Now I'm sitting there, arm bleeding, and that news hits like a brick. Everything stops. I'm not thinking about the case, the bust, none of it. Just that. That bite. Her blood, maybe in my blood.

I get rushed to the hospital. Back then, this wasn't some quick turnaround. No rapid tests. No results in 24 hours. You had to wait two weeks. Two full weeks.

And let me tell you, those were the longest damn two weeks of my life. I didn't sleep. I didn't eat right. Every little ache, I thought, that's it. That's the start. I couldn't stop thinking about my life. Did I just throw it away? All because of a $40 drug deal?

I kept showing up for work, but I was a ghost. Just going through the motions, head spinning.

Then the call came. Negative.

Negative.

I sat there in silence for a minute. Just breathing. That was the first time in two weeks I felt air in my lungs again.

After that whole mess with the bite, I stuck around to finish training Sonny. Another 30, maybe 60 days. He took to it quick—got sharp fast. Understood how to talk, how to move, how to feel the room. Before long, he was off running his own buys, doing solid work. I was proud of him.

By then, I was mostly out of undercover. Too many faces knew me, too many risks. It was time for something different.

One night, I get a call from the chief deputy over at the sheriff's office. He says, "We've got a mission in Chambers County. You in?"

Didn't take me long to say yes.

See, down in Chambers, they've got these old white shell roads. Made out of crushed oyster shells. At night, under a little moonlight, those roads lit up like runways. You could see 'em clear as day from the sky.

Turns out, that's exactly what was happening.

Small planes, helicopters—flying in from offshore rigs, from overseas, God knows where—coming in low and quiet, no lights. Landing right there on the shell roads. They'd kick out duffel bags—30, 40, 50 pounds of weed—and be back in the air before anyone heard a thing.

So the chief deputy puts this whole mission together—real serious stuff. The plan was, we were actually gonna try to catch one of these drops in real time. Not just hear about it after the fact, not scoop up the leftovers. *Catch 'em in the act.*

To get ready for that, they sent me to train with the U.S. Army Rangers.

Now, keep in mind—the military can't make arrests on U.S. soil. They can assist, sure, but they don't have that legal authority. That's where I came in. I was the cop with the badge, the one who could slap on the cuffs.

So they dropped me in with these special forces guys. They were the muscle, the movement, the silent approach. I was the one who could make it legal. And honestly, I needed them. No way I was going to catch these kinds of operators on my own.

We were gearing up for something a lot bigger than a street corner dope deal.

So there we were, way out in the middle of nowhere—flat land stretching in every direction, nothing but the dark sky above and the soft squelch of our boots in the mud. Me and five Army Rangers, moving slow and quiet through Southeast Texas rice fields, cutting across marsh. We had the intel—a plane was set to land about a mile and a half from us, and we were closing in.

Then we hit it—a canal, maybe fifteen or twenty feet across, black water under the night vision glow. I figured it had to be six, maybe eight feet deep. We stood there on the bank, staring at it, time ticking down. The urgency hit hard. The word came— twenty minutes until touchdown. If we didn't cross now, we'd lose the chance. We were burning minutes we didn't have.

Night vision on, gear strapped tight, we knew what came next. We had to get across.

I spotted him first—ten feet of alligator stretched out on the far bank, still as stone under the night vision. Just laying there, minding his business. Problem was, he was parked exactly where we needed to come out of the water.

I turned to the Rangers. "Hey, there's an alligator right there, but listen—no big deal. We've gotta cross this."

They all shifted their gaze toward him just in time to see him slide into the water and disappear. That's when the mood changed.

These were battle-tested men—guys who'd been through firefights, blown doors, worked in places where every shadow could kill you. But they'd never been told to wade through a canal with a 10-foot alligator somewhere underneath. And that night, they made it real clear—they weren't getting in that water.

I told them I'd dealt with alligators before—just shuffle your feet and get across. But the mission was hanging by a thread now. Fifteen minutes of tense back-and-forth, radio chatter pressing us, and no one willing to step in.

I finally waded in first, splashing loud, telling them I'd draw the gator's attention. Still took another fifteen minutes to get one Ranger to even dip a toe.

Eventually, the urgency pushed them in. We crossed. The gator surfaced fifty, sixty yards away—never came for us. But that night I learned something simple: people are scared of alligators.

After a few more missions like that, I finally had a little breathing room—and I asked Tiffany to marry me. We'd only been engaged six or seven months when I decided we should just get it done. Small wedding at her parents' house. Her grandfather, the justice of the peace who'd helped me get the Chambers County job, married us himself.

Life felt good. But those missions, that constant time away, had a price.

Not long after, before my transfer to drug interdiction on the highways, I was still home more often. But once we started catching traffickers on the interstate, my role shifted—follow the trail. Find out where the load came from, where it was headed.

That meant travel. And just after getting married, I was gone again—two weeks out of every month—arresting traffickers in different states with the FBI, DEA, and Customs, all across the country.

After our short wedding and brief stretch of peace, I came home one day from West Palm Beach, Florida, fresh off a drug deal there. Tiffany's face told me before her words did—something wasn't right. She sat me on the edge of the bed.

"You know, Gary," she said quietly, "I never pictured it would be like this."

I asked what she meant.

She told me she'd thought that getting out of the military would mean I'd settle down, that I'd be here. Instead, I'd taken a job that pulled me away even more. "That's just not what I pictured," she said. Then came the words that stuck—she sometimes wondered what divorce would be like.

When she said it, the picture was drawn in my mind. I began to wonder, too—what it would be like to live alone, to work until two or three in the morning with no one lying awake, worrying.

A couple of days later, I went to my district attorney and asked if he could help me file for divorce. We sat with it for a while, turned it over in our minds, and decided against it. We told ourselves we could work this out, that we could make it.

And for the next three or four months, things were great.

One day, the commander of the Narcotics Task Force called and asked if I could pick up his son from high school. I was already in my undercover car and told him sure. I also happened to be picking up Tiffany from her job around that same time, so she rode with me.

We pulled up to the school and picked up the boy—eleventh grade, seventeen years old, son of a man who'd been a policeman for fifteen or twenty years. Driving him home, I stopped for gas. I got out, walked toward the store, and heard a faint pow.

I turned and saw smoke filling my police car. My service weapon—locked in its holster behind the driver's seat—was now in the boy's hands. He'd pulled the trigger. The .45 ACP hollow point went through the back seat, just right of Tiffany's spine, entered her rib cage, tracked along a rib, and exited through the door handle.

I ran to the car, saw what had happened, and got on the radio—shot fired, accidental discharge, en route to the hospital. Chambers County lit up: sheriff's deputies, EMS, everyone headed there. I didn't wait for paramedics.

At the hospital doors, I was yelling, screaming—my wife had been shot. They calmed me down, got her into surgery. Ninety minutes later, the doctor explained: the seat foam had compressed, slowing the hollow point and keeping it from exploding. It traveled in, around her rib, and out—no rib fracture, no vessel damage.

Unbelievable. At the time, I didn't even realize just how lucky we were.

My commander arrived at the hospital, his son with him—the same 17-year-old who'd pulled the trigger. I walked straight up and hit that kid in the mouth as hard as I could.

Why? He'd been around law enforcement, around guns. Why would he touch a police officer's weapon?

The commander didn't get mad. He knew his son had that one coming.

Tiffany made a full recovery—no loss of feeling, no permanent damage. Luckiest thing I'd ever seen. A little higher, the bullet would've hit her head. A little lower, her stomach.

But after that day—after the commander's own son had done this—things in Chambers County were never the same. And neither were things between Tiffany and me.

A few months later, she told me the crazy life of undercover narcotics was more than she could handle. She didn't have to say it twice. I knew. I'd lived it too. It was time to turn the page.

Sixty-one days later, we were divorced.

Chapter 7
Second Chances

After the accident and the divorce, Chambers County wasn't the same. I knew it was time to move on. When Jefferson County called about a new jail built on military discipline, it felt like the right step—a chance to start fresh, to put structure where there was none. I didn't know then how far the program would go, or that one ordinary trip to a grocery store would change my life in ways I couldn't imagine.

The captain explained they were building something different: metal dorms with forty-four bunks in each, open bays instead of rows of cells. They wanted someone who could bring military discipline into the place. That made sense to me. I'd spent enough time working narcotics to know what lack of discipline did to people, and I knew I didn't want to go back to that world.

I thought about the families I had seen torn up by drugs— kids who didn't have food, parents who couldn't stay clean. I'd told myself I could change it, but the truth was I couldn't stop people from using. What I could do was maybe help a man straighten himself out while he was in jail. That was something I could get behind.

I toured the new facility, walked the dorms, and looked at all that empty space. It was plain—steel bunks, concrete floors— but I thought, yeah, I can work with this. I sat on it for a couple of weeks, even drove up to East Texas to see my dad and clear my head. When I came back, I put in the application. I didn't know if it would lead to a patrol job down the road or something else, but I knew I didn't want narcotics again.

When the jail finally opened and they started bringing inmates in, I took the job. The first few weeks were mostly long shifts—watching men get assigned bunks, keeping order while everyone settled in. But as I stood there in those bays, day after day, one thing kept bothering me: the inmates weren't doing anything. They just sat there.

For weeks it was the same routine. The inmates came in, got their bunks, and I worked ten-hour shifts while things settled. But the more I watched, the more it ate at me. These men sat around in their bays, eating commissary, watching TV, and sleeping when they wanted. No movement forward. No discipline beyond the bare minimum. I thought, what a waste of time and human potential.

After about thirty days, I knew I had to act. These were county inmates, not lifers. Most of them were going back to the community eventually, and they were leaving here no better than when they walked in. That didn't sit right with me. So I came up with an idea: get them into classes—something useful. Teach them how to balance a checkbook, deal with anger, pick up basic skills they could actually carry outside.

The problem was money. Somebody had to pay for the instructors and materials. That's when it hit me—use inmate labor. If we could get them producing something inside the jail, something we could sell on the outside, the revenue could cover the cost of their own rehabilitation. It was simple: make them responsible for funding their own progress.

From there we built it out. We set up levels—one through four—and called the whole thing Positive Production. But before a man could even step into Level One, we put him through a six-week boot camp. Structure first, discipline first. Only then could he start the climb.

I moved up quick through the ranks with this idea. It worked. We opened a wood shop inside the jail, and the inmates started making furniture and Christmas yard ornaments. We set up a little spot out front of the jail to sell it, and the money went right back into the rehabilitation program. It paid for uniforms, the light bill, all the things the taxpayers had been covering before. Now, instead of sitting idle, these men were working, producing, giving back. That's why we called it Positive Production.

The program went deeper than I could've imagined. I even got the chance to go back to the United States Air Force and take twelve of my correctional officers with me. We spent eight weeks in San Antonio training under their drill instructors. That changed everything. We came back sharp, organized, and the inmates responded. They respected it, and they bought into it.

The real test came not long after, when our community got hit with a terrible flood. I took forty-five inmates out into neighborhoods where water was four feet deep in homes. We sent them in to help rescue families, to carry out belongings, to keep people safe. Sometimes they had to be on their own, unsupervised, and not once did we have a problem. They understood the trust we gave them, and they honored it.

That success made people take notice. The program grew so popular that I was asked to help set it up in other places—Reno,

Nevada, Midland County, Texas, and several others across the country. Everywhere it went, it worked the same way: productive inmates, stronger communities, and a system that finally made sense.

Normally the program wasn't much of a risk, not to the sheriff's office and not to the community. The only real risk came at level four, where we trusted an inmate to leave for work during the day and then report back on time. Part of that deal was they paid 25% of their income back to the county jail as rent. It worked well, but of course, it wasn't without its dangers.

One evening, I got the call that one of our level four inmates hadn't returned. He was due back around five, but by six he still hadn't shown up. That was it—our first official escape. Now, it might sound strange calling it an escape when we were the ones who let them out, but the rule was clear: if you weren't back within the hour, you were an escapee. No exceptions.

His name was Kevin Riley. I knew his job, I knew where his parents lived, so I got into uniform, grabbed my weapons, and went to work. I checked a few places, no luck. Finally, I knocked on his mama's door. The moment she answered, I could see it in her eyes—Kevin was there. She was polite, let me search, but I didn't find him inside. I almost left, but something told me to look under the house.

It was a pier-and-beam place, maybe two and a half feet off the ground. I grabbed my shotgun, laid down on my belly, and shined my light underneath. At first, I thought I saw a piece of string. Then I realized it was a shoelace, tied to a foot. Kevin was hiding under there. Sunset was falling, and I didn't know what he had—if he was armed, if he was desperate enough to do something foolish.

I called out, steady as I could: "Kevin, don't make me shoot you. Don't make me kill you right here in front of your mom. Just come out. Let's go back to jail." He knew the score. Policy said if you escaped, you went straight to the Texas Department of Criminal Justice. No more trustee status, no more chances. State prison is a hard place, and he knew it.

For twenty minutes I waited him out, deputies arriving to back me up. Finally, I got through to him. He crawled out, I cuffed him, and I hauled him straight back—not to the barracks, but to Maximum Security, where he stayed until the state came to get him.

That was one failure. But for every Kevin Riley, there were hundreds of successes. To this day, my wife and I can walk into a Walmart or a restaurant, and half the time a former inmate will come up, shake my hand, and say, "You saved my life. That was the hardest thing I ever did, but it changed me." And I'll tell you—that is a beautiful feeling.

Still, running that program was stressful. The responsibility never left your shoulders. I carried the weight of a whole community's safety, and every decision fell back on me. When I cleared an inmate for work release, that was mine alone. Nobody else signed off.

To deal with the pressure, I leaned on friends from the sheriff's office and the police department. We'd kick back, watch a football game or a baseball game, fire up the pit, and just let things go for a while.

One evening we were into a Cowboys game, barbecue pit going, drinks poured, when we ran out of food. I told the guys I'd run up to the corner store and grab some sausage links. Nothing special, just a quick errand. But standing in line at that little grocery store, I noticed the cashier—a petite blonde with a name tag that read "Samantha." She looked young, and I was already twenty-six, so I hesitated at first. But as she rang up my groceries, we slipped into easy conversation. About the game, the barbecue, just small talk that seemed to carry on longer than it should've, with a line of folks waiting behind me.

Before I walked off, I asked what time she got off. "Six-thirty," she said. I half-joked that she ought to swing by—we'd still be barbecuing. Honestly, I didn't expect anything to come of it. But sure enough, around quarter to seven, a car I didn't recognize pulled into my driveway. Out stepped Samantha, still in her grocery store uniform, smiling like she belonged there.

That night we talked, we laughed, we traded numbers. It was simple and easy, nothing forced. At the time, I thought it was just a chance meeting. Looking back, I realize it was the beginning of something much bigger. I had no way of knowing that girl behind the checkout counter would end up being my second wife.

Sometimes the biggest turns in life don't come from the decisions that weigh the heaviest—but from a quick trip to the store.

Chapter 8
New Babies

Life has a way of shifting when you least expect it. One day, I was buried in the routine — work, responsibilities, the usual nights with the guys — and the next, things started moving faster than I could keep up with. Meeting Samantha felt simple at first, like any chance encounter, but it wouldn't stay that way for long. Before I knew it, life was changing — new love, new responsibilities, and more blessings than I ever thought I'd be ready for.

I took the job with the Federal Bureau of Prisons, and they sent me to Georgia for four weeks of training. While I was there, I called Samantha and had her fly out for a couple of days. Everything felt good — new job, new wife, a fresh start. After she flew home, I finished up training and came back ready to settle in.

About three months in, Samantha and I went out for a nice dinner. In the middle of the meal, she reaches into her purse, pulls out what looks like a little plastic popsicle, and sets it on the table. Clear as day, there's a red line in the middle. She looks at me and says, "We're pregnant." All I could manage was, "Oh boy." Just a few months into marriage and we were already getting ready for the next chapter.

At the time, we were still living with her dad, but with a baby on the way, I knew it was time to get a place of our own. We bought our first house and got everything ready for the baby. A few months later, Callie was born — a healthy little girl. Life was good.

A couple of years into the job, I made supervisor. Things kept moving forward, so we decided to build a new house. By the time it was finished and we were ready to move in, Samantha was pregnant again. This time with a boy — we named him Kyle. Brand-new house, two kids, a good job — everything felt like it was falling into place.

Then reality came knocking. One evening, I'd just settled in at home — maybe half an hour after my shift — when the phone rang. It was close to six, and the voice on the other end was calm but clipped: the prison was on lockdown. A fight had been brewing all day, and it was about to blow wide open. They wanted everyone in.

By the time I pulled through the gates, the place felt different — quiet, but not the kind of quiet you want. The briefing was short and sharp: chow time was about to turn ugly, and we needed to be ready. The Federal Bureau of Prisons unit I worked in held 3,300 inmates. Big place. Big problems.

We lined up just outside the chow hall, radios clipped and body alarms ready. When the first alarm went off, it didn't just sound — it screamed. We charged in, and it was chaos. Plates flying, tables tipped, inmates swinging at each other like it was a war zone. And then the second round of alarms went off — another housing unit had erupted.

As a supervisor, I didn't have the luxury of freezing. I grabbed six or seven officers, and we ran. The second I rounded the corner, I felt the air shift, and instinct made me duck. Whack! A lock in a sock swung right over my head — inches from catching me clean. They'd been waiting for us.

The riot was full-blown. The inmates weren't after us, not really. We were just in the way of whatever scores they were settling. But that didn't make it any less dangerous. Blood slicked the floors, radios screamed with overlapping calls, and every second stretched out like an hour.

It took six long hours to get control back. By the end of it, staff were being wheeled out on stretchers, several heading to the hospital. A few inmates never made it out. Ugly doesn't begin to cover it.

When the dust settled, I knew I was done with the frontline. I'd put in my time, taken the hits, but something in me had shifted. The next opening that came up, I took — still inside the prison, but away from the chaos. They needed someone to oversee the industrial program, teaching inmates how to make Kevlar helmets for the military. With my background, I was a natural fit.

It wasn't a clean break from the job, but it was a change. After that night, I figured I'd earned one.

That job went on for several years without a hitch. It was steady work — good pay, good insurance, good for the family. But after a while, I just got bored. That's all there was to it.

So, on my breaks at the prison, I started listening. Not to music, not to talk radio — to coyotes. Yeah, coyotes. Out in our community, on the farms and ranches, we'd been having real problems with them attacking deer and livestock, and for some reason, that got stuck in my head.

I decided I wanted to understand them — to know exactly what they were saying to each other. So I dove in. I listened to everything I could find, learned all I could about their behavior, their sounds, their calls. And when I'd get off my shift at the prison, I'd take my boat down to one of the local bayous, cut the motor, and just sit there in the dark. I'd listen to the different packs talking across the water, trying to figure out what each call meant.

Before long, I started trying to talk back. Took an old duck call I had, tore it apart, shaved the reed down, reworked it until it sounded like one of them. Night after night, I'd listen to my recordings and fine-tune the sound. Eventually, I got to where I could match their voices — their commands, their warnings — almost perfectly.

Turned out, I was good at it. Real good. My calls worked so well that word got around fast. Before I knew it, the calls I'd been building in my garage were hanging on the racks in hunting stores all over the country.

Then I figured, why stop there? Making the calls was good, but if folks wanted to learn, I could take them out and show them how it's done. So now, not only was I building the calls, but I was also running hunts at night. It got busy fast. I'd get off at the federal prison at five, grab a bite, and by seven I'd be back in the truck, taking people out until one or two in the morning. Then, right back to work the next day. It was exhausting, but I loved every bit of it.

One night, I had some customers with me. We were set up on the bank of a bayou, calling. The water slid by in the moonlight, quiet, like it always is right before something happens. We could hear coyotes working through the woods on the far side, and we were watching through the night vision, waiting for them to break loose.

Then it happened — the water just exploded. Out comes this ten-foot alligator, and before we could even move, he snatched a young calf that was standing there getting a drink. Took it straight back into the water like it was nothing.

Right then, I knew I wasn't just hunting coyotes anymore. We had an alligator problem. What I didn't realize at that moment was that watching that big gator grab that calf was about to put me on the path to my next twenty-five-year career.

After that night, I went over to some new land to ask permission to hunt coyotes. I saw this place that looked like it stretched for miles — plenty of open ground behind the house — so I figured it was worth a try. I parked the truck, walked up to the door, and knocked.

This guy comes to the door, a tall, clean-cut fella, maybe a few years older than me. He looked at me like he wasn't sure what I wanted, so I told him straight. "Sir," I said, "we've got a growing coyote problem in this area, and I'd like to know if I could get permission to hunt on your land."

He studied me for a second, sizing me up, then said, "You sure can — but only under one condition."

I said, "What's that?"

He grinned. "If I get to go with you."

I laughed. "Deal."

His name was Jay Francis, and right then I had no idea that knock on his door was about to turn into a real friendship. Over the next couple of days — and nights — Jay and I ran his land, hunting coyotes together. We managed to take out a few of them, which helped, but more than that, we just clicked. Jay was one of those guys you felt like you'd known for years after just an hour of talking.

One night, while we were sitting out there, waiting and watching, I told him, "You know, the other night, I was over at another place, and I watched an alligator come right up out of the water and grab a baby calf."

Jay's eyes got wide. "You're kidding me."

"Nope. Dragged that calf right under like it was nothing."

Jay shook his head. "Well, you know during gator season, I hunt alligators."

I looked at him. "Really?"

"Yeah," he said, leaning back against the truck. "I'll show you how to get tags for them."

Sure enough, Jay walked me through how to approach the state of Texas and get legal tags. I went to the landowner who'd lost that calf, told him what I planned to do, and he agreed to let me hunt the gators on his place. That season, I got ten tags for the meat and the skins.

Since I was already running guided hunts for coyotes, it didn't take long for the word to get around. Folks wanted to try their hand at catching an alligator, and I sold every single one of those tags that year. Ten out of ten, gone.

Here's how it worked: we'd take the customer out, hang chicken over the bayou water with a heavy line and a big shark hook. The gator would take the bait during the night, swallow it whole, and by morning it'd still be hooked. Then I'd bring the customer out, we'd pull the line tight, haul the gator up, and they'd shoot it.

Now, I'll tell you, that part never sat right with me. I don't mind hunting — I've always believed if you do it quick and clean, it's fair. But this? This wasn't that. That hook didn't just catch in their mouth; they swallowed it. That big number nine shark hook would be buried deep in their stomach, and they'd spend the whole night pulling against it, tearing themselves up inside. Then you'd show up in the morning, drag them out, and finally put them down.

I did it that one year because I'd committed to it and had customers counting on me, but it just wasn't for me. I didn't like the thought of something suffering like that, all night long, just because someone paid for the thrill of it. So when that season ended, I was done with gator hunts.

Around that same time, I was still living in a quiet little neighborhood. One evening during gator season, I had an alligator in the back of my truck that a customer had harvested. I'd just backed into the driveway — tailgate down, gator stretched out across the bed — when this kid from down the street comes buzzing around the corner on his ATV.

He slows down, eyes wide, staring at the truck bed. "Where'd you get that alligator?" he says.

I said, "Not around here. Got him off a different piece of land."

The kid shakes his head. "Well, have you ever seen the alligator that's right down the road?"

I looked at him like he'd just grown a second head. "What are you talking about?"

"Yeah," he says, "there's an old abandoned alligator farm not a mile from here."

I just stood there. "I've never even heard of it."

He grins. "Tell you what. Grab your ATV, follow me, and I'll show you."

I didn't know it at the time, but that ride was gonna change the next twenty-five years of my life.

I climbed on my ATV, cranked it up, and followed him down this old, beat-up trail off the main highway. The path was so overgrown you could hardly see the ground in front of you. Old sagging fences ran along the sides, rusted wire hanging loose. After about a mile, the trail opened up a bit, and the kid pulls up to this faded fence line. Grass was as tall as his shoulders, weeds everywhere.

He hops off his ATV, grabs a five-gallon bucket sitting by the fence, and picks up a stick lying next to it. Then he starts banging on that bucket.

I cut my engine and holler, "Hey, what are you doing?"

He just grins and says, "Hang on. You're about to understand what this is."

He keeps banging — bang, bang, bang — until suddenly he stops. "Listen," he says.

And that's when I hear it. At first, just the faint sound of water splashing somewhere beyond the fence. Then — crack. Snap. Heavy sticks breaking, one after another, like something big was moving through the brush.

Then I see it. The grass starts parting, two feet wide, like somebody dragging a log through it. My first thought was, what in the world is this? Felt like something out of a dinosaur movie.

Then I see the tip of a snout. One slow step. Then another. And another.

That's when I first laid eyes on him — Big Al.

That alligator was massive. Thirteen feet, four inches of pure muscle and attitude. I swear, when he eased up to that old fence and laid there, it was like time stopped. His head alone looked like it could swallow a basketball.

I looked at the kid and said, "What are you doing? Why are you banging that bucket?"

He said, "Normally, we bring him food. When this was a farm, that's what they did — they fed him. He's just waiting to eat."

I was still trying to take it all in when I hear the brush moving again, just behind Big Al.

And here she comes.

Another gator, not quite as big but meaner — quicker. I looked down and noticed there was a hole in the fence.

And that's when my stomach dropped.

Because while Big Al was staying put, she wasn't. She slid right under that hole in the fence like it was nothing, and suddenly it was me, this kid, and a full-grown alligator standing way too close.

I turned to the kid and said, "Get back on your ATV. Now."

I had nothing — no rope, no stick, nothing but my hands. And here comes this gator, head low, eyes locked on us.

I waited until she got just close enough, then lunged, grabbed her tail, and spun her around with everything I had.

By the grace of God, she spun back toward the hole in that fence and, thank goodness, walked right back in.

We didn't waste a second. We got out of there, went straight into town, bought some raw chicken, and came right back.

Fed Big Al and that female — who I'd later learn was his mate, Allie.

That moment hooked me. Those two giants had been abandoned out there for seven years, surviving on their own. And right then and there, standing by that broken-down fence with two alligators waiting to be fed, I knew I had to figure out how to own that old abandoned alligator farm.

After we fed Big Al and Allie that first day, something just clicked in me. I don't know how to explain it, but I knew — this was what I wanted to do. I wanted to spend my life with these animals, to build something that gave them a place and gave people a chance to see them up close.

The old farm wasn't far off the highway, and I kept thinking, if I can clean this place up, rebuild it, bring it back to life, people will come. Folks will drive out here to see the American alligator, to understand it. So I tracked down the landowner, knocked on his door, and told him what I wanted to do. I said, "I don't have the money to buy it right now, but if you'd lease it to me, I'd do the work on my time, my money, my sweat. Give me one year, and if I can make it work, I'll buy it from you."

He agreed — said I could lease it — and even reminded me there were alligators back there, like that was supposed to scare me off. I just smiled and said, "That's exactly what I want. I want the alligators, and I want the land."

So that's what I did. I was still working my shifts at the Federal Bureau of Prisons, Monday through Thursday, ten hours a day. Fridays, Saturdays, Sundays — every minute was spent out at that old, broken-down farm. I was still making my coyote calls, still keeping up with orders from all over the country, but my real focus was rebuilding that place from the ground up.

I had this picture in my head of what it could be — not just a farm, but a park. A place where families could come, feed the gators safely, learn about them, and see that these animals weren't just some mindless predators in the swamp. I wanted it to be educational. I wanted kids to leave with a little more respect for what they'd seen.

It was hard — no sense lying about that. Some days I'd park an old trailer under a tree, hook up a generator to a fan, and that was my kids' air conditioning while I worked. They were just three and six years old back then, sitting there with their snacks and drinks, waving at me while I climbed up on that old tractor and pushed through the Texas heat.

And, man, people laughed. We lived in a neighborhood a mile down the road from the farm. Every morning I'd rumble down the street on that tractor, neighbors sitting on their porches with their coffee, shaking their heads. Every evening I'd come back the same way, dirt-caked, sweat-soaked, and dragging. By then they'd have their cold drinks in hand, laughing all over again. They told me I was crazy, that it would never work, that I was wasting my time and my money.

But I ignored every last one of them. I kept my head down, day after day, week after week, chasing that vision I couldn't shake. My goal was September 2005 — that was the deadline I'd set in my own head.

And sure enough, by early September, I had it ready. Decks built, systems set, everything safe and in place for the public. The dream that had lived in my head for so long was finally standing there in front of me, real as could be. All I could think was: this is it — the start of something big.

Life was finally rolling smooth — or so I thought.

Chapter 9
Storms in My Life

One morning, just like any other, I flipped on the morning news before heading out to work. The headline hit me like a gut punch: Level Four Hurricane, barreling straight for Southeast Texas.

Her name was Rita. And let me tell you, Rita wasn't just another storm — to this day, she still holds her place as one of the nastiest, most destructive hurricanes to ever slam into our part of the world.

Now, here's the kicker. I didn't just have Gator Country to worry about — which, by itself, was a full-time job when you've got animals, park structures, and a deadline to accomplish — but I also had my federal job to deal with at the Bureau of Prisons.

At the prison, we didn't have to evacuate inmates for hurricanes — thank God — but we sure as hell had to prepare for being locked down and cut off from the outside world. We knew the electricity was going down, we knew the roads were gonna be a mess, and we knew no trucks would be making deliveries for a while. That meant we had to stock up. And by "stock up," I mean load up with everything from food to medical supplies to fuel.

The warden called me in and said, "Gary, you're gonna lead the caravan."

Fifteen vehicles. Vans. A couple of 18-wheelers. Whatever we could find to haul supplies. And me, sitting in the lead truck with a radio in one hand and a map in the other, wondering what in the hell I'd gotten myself into.

The plan was simple enough: haul ass up to Texarkana, load up, and haul ass back before the storm. Except — storms have a way of laughing at your plans.

We pulled out with police escorts clearing the highways for us. Cars were backed up for miles with folks trying to get out of town. Every time I looked in the mirror, it was like watching an ocean of red brake lights behind us. It was eerie — like the whole world was running while we were driving straight into the lion's mouth.

Five hours later, we rolled into Texarkana, and the crew there didn't waste a second. They loaded us down with everything — pallets of canned goods, water, fuel, medical supplies, you name it. We were packed to the gills. And then, as if that wasn't enough, they handed us chainsaws, portable lights, and firearms.

"Why the hell do we need all this?" I thought. But I didn't ask questions. Not yet.

As Rita roared ashore, the call came from our warden in Beaumont:

"Start driving. Get those supplies back here now."

The storm wasn't even finished tearing up the coast — still a solid Category 2 — and here we were, ordered to drive right into it.

We followed orders.

About two hours from Beaumont, the reality hit. The winds were howling, trees were snapping like matchsticks, and the highways were a graveyard of fallen pine trees. And then it clicked — that's why we'd been handed chainsaws.

Every mile, we'd stop. Fire up the saws. Clear one, two, sometimes three massive trees just to get a few hundred yards down the road. The rain was coming at us sideways. The trucks were fishtailing. And every time I thought about quitting, I'd look in the rearview and see those other drivers waiting on me to keep pushing forward.

What should've been a five-hour return trip turned into a thirteen-hour crawl through hell. By the time we finally rolled through the gates of the Beaumont facility, I was exhausted, soaked to the bone, and running on fumes — but we'd done it. Supplies delivered. Mission accomplished.

With the immediate weight off my shoulders, my mind shifted straight to Gator Country. I needed to know — what kind of damage did Rita leave behind? Were my animals safe? Was the park even standing?

Before I could get answers, the warden came down with another order:

"Nobody leaves for three days. Power's out everywhere. Roads are a mess. We're staying locked down to keep things under control."

Three days.

So, while Southeast Texas tried to pick up the pieces, I sat there, waiting — anxious, restless — just wanting to get back to my park and see for myself what Rita had done.

Man, I finally got ahold of a neighbor that lived close to Gator Country. I just needed eyes on the ground — somebody to tell me I still had an alligator park standing. For a couple days, I was hanging on to hope, waiting on that call. When it finally came, it was nothing I wanted to hear.

They said it was just devastation. Those big, beautiful oak trees that used to shade the entrance? Laying across the driveway like fallen giants. Pine trees snapped in half, leaning over the fences so wide open an alligator could just crawl right out. It was a mess. A major, major catastrophe.

And the crazy thing is, I'd just built it from nothing a few months before. Every nail, every board, every hour I'd put in — it was still fresh in my hands. But this time, there was no just "rebuilding." The bathrooms, the snack shack, the gift shop — gone. Completely rolled off their piers and scattered like they'd never been there. It looked like someone had just wiped their hand clean across the whole place.

I remember sitting there, just quiet. Staring off, trying to wrap my head around it. Where do I even start? How do you rebuild when there's nothing left to rebuild from?

After that week at the Bureau, when the warden gave us time off, I finally felt like I could breathe — just for a second. It wasn't relief, not really, but at least I had time. Time to go back and see what could be done, time to try and figure out where to start.

Five months. I had been working on it for five months. I grabbed my chainsaw and told myself, one day at a time. That was all I could do. Those oak trees — God, they were massive. It took the biggest chainsaw I could find just to get through the thick trunks. I'd cut, stack the wood, and move to the next one. No rushing, no sense in that. Just slow, steady work, clearing one piece at a time.

When I finally made it up to the gift shop — what was left of it — I dug through the mess to see if anything could be saved. There wasn't much. A couple of things here and there, but mostly it was ruined. I poured gas on what was left and set it on fire. Then I just sat there, watching the flames burn it down to nothing. It felt like watching every hour I'd worked, every dollar I'd scraped together, every bit of sweat I'd poured into that place… just go up in smoke.

The bathrooms were next. They'd survived the flood somehow, but not this storm. The wind had just shredded them, crumbled them. So, I burned those too. There was no saving what was too broken to fix.

Once the ashes settled, I knew standing around feeling sorry for myself wasn't going to get the place rebuilt. If it was going to rise again, it had to start with me — one board, one nail, one day at a time.

There wasn't much money to work with, but I had good credit. So, I went down to the hardware store — Home Depot, one of those big-box places — and they handed me a $10,000 credit card. That plastic card felt like a lifeline. The money gave me a start, but the rest was going to come down to grit, sweat, and stubbornness.

That card is what rebuilt Gator Country. Ten thousand dollars, a chainsaw, and a stubborn streak. One bathroom at a time, one stick at a time. By March — months of steady, exhausting work later — I had the gates open. Not shiny, not fancy, but open.

About thirty days after we opened, we were finally starting to feel like things were moving forward at the park. By then, I'd decided we'd call it **Gator Country** — and from that day on, that's what it was. Gator Country.

We were having a little cookout there one evening. Nothing big, just frying up some fish, hanging out, celebrating the fact that we'd actually pulled this place together. There was a small building we used for cooking, and I was in there manning the fryer, grease popping, people laughing outside, kids running around — just a good evening.

Somebody said we needed something from the store, so I told them, "Alright, I'll run and get it." But before I could grab my keys, Samantha — my wife at the time — stopped me. She said, "No, no, let me go. I'll run down there." I said, "Alright, if you don't mind," and handed her the list. She headed off to the little neighborhood store just five minutes down the road.

A few minutes later, I realized I'd forgotten something. So I called her. When I did, the phone made that beeping sound, like the line was busy. She was on another call. I thought, *well, that's odd,* but didn't think too much of it.

A while passed and I still didn't hear from her, so I hung up and dialed her dad. I said, "Hey, have you heard from Samantha?" He said, "No, haven't talked to her." Then I called a buddy, nothing there either. So I called her back again, and this time she answered.

I said, "Were you just on the other line?" She said, "Yeah, I was talking to my dad."

And I thought, *huh, maybe I just called him in the middle of it.* I told her what else I needed from the store, and she said she'd grab it and head back.

But something didn't sit right. I called her dad again. I said, "Hey, did Samantha just call you?" And he said, "No, I haven't heard from her all day."

That sinking feeling hit me right in the gut. I'd been in law enforcement. I'd worked corrections. You get that instinct — that little voice that tells you when something's off — and I knew. I just knew.

She came back to the park later and walked into the building where I was still cooking, and I asked her, "Hey, who were you on the phone with?" She looked at me and said, "What are you doing, checking up on me?" Defensive. Immediately defensive.

And right there, I knew. I didn't want to know, but I knew.

We wrapped up the evening, got the kids home, got them to bed. She went straight to sleep, but I couldn't. I sat there with that sick feeling in my stomach until I finally opened up the laptop and pulled up the call records.

And there it was. A number. Not just from that night — but from the days leading up to it. Over and over, the same number.

I walked into the bedroom, woke her up, and said, "Before I call this number, I want to know who it is. I *will* find out."

And that was it. That was the beginning of something that would change everything.

I had a three-year-old and a six-year-old. I thought I was doing everything right — working hard, building a future, putting my time, my sweat, my money into something that was going to be ours. And in that moment, standing there in the dark with that phone in my hand, I realized somewhere along the way… I'd missed the boat.

That night didn't just end with betrayal. A heavy rain turned into another flood, and by the time morning came, Gator Country was under water again. I barely had time to process what I'd uncovered before the park — everything I'd built, every dollar I'd scraped together — was gutted all over. Between the storm and what I'd just learned, I was left standing there with nothing but two little kids and an empty pocket. Bankrupt in every way a man can be.

Chapter 10
Once Again

I've been through some storms in my life, but that stretch right there — the days after it all fell apart — that was a different kind. Not the kind that blows your house down, but the kind that settles heavy in your chest and won't let go. Ten days on that couch, barely moving, barely talking. The kids tiptoeing through the house like they knew something was broken, and me just staring at the ceiling, wondering how the hell I'd gotten here.

At some point, I realized I couldn't stay like that. Not with two kids depending on me. Not with life still moving, whether I was ready for it or not. Something had to give, and it sure wasn't going to be them.

I didn't have a plan. Didn't have a dollar to rub together. Just me, that couch, and a house that felt like it didn't want me in it anymore. Eight, maybe ten days I stayed there, barely speaking, just trying to figure out which way was up. Every time I passed her in the hall, it was like walking through ice.

On the tenth morning, I sat up and told myself, you can't keep doing this. It wasn't just bad for me — it was bad for the kids, and that was the only thing that mattered. So, with nothing but pride in my pocket, I picked up the phone and called a buddy of mine who'd been through his own divorce not long before. Told him straight up, "Man, I need somewhere to go." He didn't even hesitate. Said, "I've got a room — small, but it's yours." Ten by ten, maybe. Four walls, a bed, and just enough space to breathe. It wasn't much, but at that moment, it was everything.

Then reality hit me like a hammer. I needed a lawyer. I needed to figure out how to keep my kids' lives as normal as possible. And I still had to clock in at the federal prison every day, still had Gator Country to rebuild, and still had customers booking coyote hunts at night. It was too much. Something had to give.

That's when I let the coyote business go. That one hurt. I'd built it from the ground up, put everything I had into it, but holding onto it meant I was drowning. Selling it turned out to be the right call, though, because that money gave me just enough to put a down payment on a little mobile home. Had it moved onto the property at Gator Country so I'd have a place for my kids when they were with me.

The divorce dragged on, and when it finally wrapped, the judge handed down the standard setup — every other weekend and Wednesday nights, plus a child support payment that felt impossible with what I was making. I hated it. That wasn't the deal I thought I'd signed up for when I said "I do." But I made sure I was there. Every morning, every afternoon — dropping the kids off, picking them up, even on the days they weren't technically mine.

After a while, I started to notice something. I was spending more time with them than she was. That didn't make sense, not to me and sure as hell not to them. Divorce is a disease like that — spreads through the whole family, and the kids catch the worst of it. So I asked her straight up, "Let's do 50-50. They deserve that. We deserve that." She pitched a fit, of course, so I took her back to court.

And I won.

I can't tell you the relief that brought. Not because of the money — though easing up on that child support meant I could finally buy my kids what they needed without asking anyone for help — but because it felt like validation. Like the judge was saying what I already knew: I was that good of a dad.

And just like that, we moved forward.

Then, right when I thought maybe things were settling, I find out who Samantha had the affair with. And it just drops me flat when I hear the name. It's somebody I work with. Somebody I see every single day when I walk through that gate. My brain goes to a whole another level. Now, not only am I trying to keep my head straight with the kids and the house and everything else, but I've got to walk past this guy every day like nothing happened.

It was the worst feeling in the world, I'm telling you. It wasn't just that he took my wife — he took time with my kids. Two weeks after I moved out, this guy moved right in. Same bed, same TV, same everything. No pride. Just slid right into my house like he belonged there. Every thought of it burned.

I'd walk into that prison, and the second I'd see him, I'd feel it in my chest. I had to find a way to keep my cool, because I knew what would happen if I didn't. Finally, I went to my warden. I sat down in his office and laid it out straight: told him I was having some really bad feelings, that I didn't trust myself in that situation. He just sat there quiet for a minute, then he told me, "You're good at what you do. Don't let this mess ruin that. Don't do something you can't take back."

That talk helped. It didn't fix it — not by a long shot — but it gave me enough to keep moving, to keep my head down and do my job. But I'll be honest, those days were some of the hardest I've ever had. Walking past him, pretending like it was just another day, when all I wanted to do was… well, you know.

Days keep rolling by, and on my days off, I'm still out at Gator Country, trying to rebuild everything. One day, I'm out there in the heat — middle of June, one of those Texas summer days where the air feels like it's cooking you alive. I'm working on this metal fence, got the grinder going, sparks flying everywhere, and I'm holding that thing tight, trying to cut through a piece of pipe.

Then, out of nowhere, I start itching. And not just a little itch — it's like fire crawling under my skin. Under my arms, down the side of my neck, all over my ribs. And the more I sweat, the worse it gets. I finally stop, wipe the sweat off my face, and when I look down, my whole side is bright red, covered in hives. I couldn't figure out what in the world was going on, but every minute it's getting worse, like something's eating me alive.

I had to put the grinder down and haul myself to urgent care. Soon as the doctor saw me, he didn't hesitate. He said, "Scabies." Now, I didn't know much about scabies at the time, but I knew enough to know I didn't like the sound of it. Basically, it's a type of lice, and it's nasty. Makes you itch like crazy, and the more you scratch, the worse it spreads.

Turns out, I picked it up at work — at the prison. Back when I was in the factory, making Kevlar helmets, the inmates had to take their shoes off at the end of every shift to make sure nobody was carrying out any shanks or tools. My job was to slide their shoes down the line, every single day. Come to find out, that's where I got it.

Now, a couple days with the cream and the powder knocked it out, but man, I'm telling you, that was one of the most miserable things I've ever dealt with. It was like being on fire and itching all over at the same time. And to have that piled on top of everything else I was going through? Felt like life was just seeing how much more I could take.

Months roll by, and before I know it, the house is delivered. Three bedrooms — nothing fancy, but it worked. I had my room, and my two kids each had their own. Watching them run through the place that first day was something. They were happy, and that was good enough for me.

The divorce got finalized, and life started to settle. My head was clearer. We got into a routine — school, work, home — just the normal day-to-day.

Fridays turned into my favorite day. I'd take a little time to have lunch with the kids at their school, sit with them in the cafeteria, hear their stories. I made it to their games and activities when I could, always trying to be there.

Every now and then, I'd step out. Hit a dance club one weekend, maybe a honky-tonk the next. Nothing serious, just getting back out there, remembering what it felt like to have a little fun.

Attitude was good. Life was steady. And for the first time in a long time, things just felt… alright.

And even with life leveling out, I couldn't shake the thought of that place — Gator Country. I'd poured too much of myself into it to let the floods have the last word. Every time I drove past the land, I saw more than ruins; I saw what it could be again. It wasn't going to be quick or easy, but I was willing to start over, one board, one nail, one day at a time.

The truth was, I was running on empty. Every dollar I'd saved, every credit card, every bit of credit I could squeeze out — it was all tied up in the park. I'd been leasing the property for a year, and the clock was running out. If I wanted Gator Country to survive, I had to find a way to buy that land. And buying it meant one thing: walking into a bank and asking for more money than I'd ever dreamed of borrowing.

I'd made a deal with the owner early on: if I could make it work in a year, I'd buy it. Simple as that. But just as we started moving forward, the storms hit — one after another. By the time that first year was up, I'd already rebuilt twice, patching together what the wind and water kept tearing apart.

By mid-2006, every card I had was maxed out. No savings. No safety net. Nothing but grit and stubbornness holding it together. It was time to swallow my pride and ask for help.

So, I walked into a local bank with my idea, laid it all out: an alligator park. For tourists. For kids. Educational, too. They didn't even let me finish before laughing me right out the door.

Walking back to my truck that day, I felt like someone had kicked me straight in the gut. I remember thinking, What now? I'd poured everything into that place. I couldn't just walk away.

So, I tried another bank. This time, they didn't laugh. They actually listened — but they still said no. Not yet, anyway.

They told me, "We don't think a standalone alligator park is going to make it. Think of something else you can add, something to bring people in and keep them coming back. Then come see us in a week."

I didn't leave that meeting with my head down. No, this time my mind was racing. What can I tell them that'll get me that million-dollar loan? Didn't matter what it was — if that's what they needed to hear, I'd find a way to tell it.

I went straight to work. Talked to the Economic Development Center, the Chamber of Commerce — anybody who would give me five minutes. And that's when it hit me: a restaurant.

Picture this — a bridge over the alligator enclosure, leading to a 200-seat restaurant. Great food, great views, a one-of-a-kind experience you couldn't get anywhere else. I didn't care a bit about running a restaurant — but I cared about saving Gator Country.

It took two weeks to build the business plan — numbers, projections, every last detail they'd want to see. And when I walked back into that bank and laid it all out, they nodded. Approved it.

One million dollars.

They financed the land. They financed the building. I scraped together what little cash I could and signed the papers. Next thing I knew, we were putting up an 8,800-square-foot restaurant.

Here's the truth — I had no idea what I was doing. I wasn't a restaurant guy. I caught gators. But I knew this: if I wanted to keep my park alive, that restaurant had to work.

Building it was its own nightmare. Bad contractors. Stolen materials. Money disappearing. Every day there was a new fire to put out. But six months later, somehow, we got the doors open. It was nothing but a wing and a prayer, but I told myself, Give it your best shot. See where it lands.

I wasn't ready for what came next.

People showed up in droves. No, you don't understand — opening day, we were supposed to open at five in the evening, just for dinner. By four o'clock, there was already a line. We were on a two-hour wait before the doors even unlocked.

It was phenomenal. And terrifying.

I had fifty-three employees in that building, and from the first night, it was chaos. Orders flying, servers crashing into each other, customers complaining about food or the wait — everything happening all at once.

And I hated it. Every bit of it. I can wrestle a gator in the middle of a swamp without blinking, but a restaurant full of angry customers glaring over cold fries or long waits? That wasn't my world.

But I didn't have a choice. I had to make it work.

And it wasn't just the stress. Employees were stealing — food, money, whatever they thought they could get away with. And all the while, the park still needed me. The gators still had to be fed, the maintenance done, the tours run. It was like juggling fire while standing in quicksand.

Then, in the middle of all that chaos, came a blessing.

One Saturday morning, just after we'd opened the park, a family came through the gates. The boy — fourteen, maybe — lit up the second he saw the alligators. He followed his parents around for hours, feeding the gators, holding the babies, asking question after question.

By the end of the day, when we were locking up, they were still there. That's when his mom walked over and said, "He's so infatuated with these alligators… he'd love to work here. Even if it's just mowing grass, just to be around them."

I smiled, took her number, figured it was just something parents say when their kid's got a new obsession. But a few weeks later, when the grass was knee-high and the trash needed hauling, I remembered that number.

His name was Damon. And for a fourteen-year-old, he was a giant — six-two, two hundred pounds, towering over me like a grown man. But underneath it all, he was just a kid with stars in his eyes.

Every Saturday, he'd mow the grass, trim the edges, take out the trash, wash dishes in the little restaurant — and the second the work was done, he'd disappear into the park, hanging around the gators. Always careful. Always respectful. But you could see that spark every time.

That summer, he never missed a weekend.

Then one day, his dad came to me, looking worn thin. He said, "Gary, we're not doing well. I'm having a hard time feeding Damon. The drive out here every weekend… it's too much. Is there any way he could stay here on the weekends instead of me driving forty miles one way?"

I didn't hesitate. "I've got an extra room," I told him. "He can stay."

And just like that, Damon started spending weekends at Gator Country. When school started back, he'd head home during the week, but every Friday night, there he was — ready to work, ready to be around the gators.

And it didn't stop after that first summer.

For three straight years, Damon was there every weekend. Somewhere along the way, he stopped being just a kid helping out. He became family — my third child.

What I didn't know then was that one day, Damon would marry my daughter. And that same boy, the one who started out mowing grass just to be near the alligators, would go on to save my life.

By 2008, life finally started to level out. The restaurant was holding steady, the park was bringing in good crowds, and for the first time in a long while, I could actually breathe.

I even had time to coach my son's flag football team. And then, thanks to my daughter — without asking me — I ended up coaching her soccer team, too. Had to pick a team name and everything. I went with the Running Coyotes. Sounded tough enough.

Only problem? I didn't know a thing about soccer. Not one thing.

First game rolls around, and my daughter's sprinting down the field like it's track practice. She stops, looks right at me, and yells, "Dad, soccer ain't for me!"

And there I was — stuck coaching a full season of a sport I didn't understand, for a kid who'd already quit in her head. But we stuck it out, played every game, and even won a few. Looking back, it was frustrating, sure — but it was fun.

Life felt… good. Balanced, even. I was working hard, but I was finding time to live a little — going out honky-tonking, having a date or two. Nothing serious, just a chance to feel normal again.

Then the phone rang.

It was a call from a show called River Monsters on Animal Planet. They told me Jeremy Wade, the host, wanted to come down and film an episode right there at Gator Country. National TV.

I can't lie — I was over the moon. So much so that I forgot about the VIP tickets I'd gotten for a Houston Texans game that weekend. Front-row seats. I'd promised to take my boy. Felt awful telling him I couldn't go, but I knew this was something big.

So, I handed the tickets to his grandpa, and off they went. He came back grinning ear to ear, talking a mile a minute about the game. Meanwhile, I stayed at the park, knee-deep in what I didn't realize would be the start of something huge.

We filmed the show, and it blew up. Reran over 200 times. People still tell me they saw me on that first episode of River Monsters. It was good — really good — for the park, for business, for everything. And it was just the beginning. Over the next few years, I'd go on to do more than seventy-five national TV shows.

But after the cameras packed up, it was back to reality. Back in the restaurant, apron on, keeping the lights on and the bills paid.

Then came the morning that reminded me just how fragile it all was.

We were doing closeouts from the night before. The cash was counted, deposits ready, the money locked in the safe. My office manager pulled out $3,500, put it in a money bag, and left it on her desk for just a minute while she ran to the restroom.

When she came back, the bag was gone.

$3,500.

That was a lot of money for a brand-new business like ours. My stomach just sank.

I locked the building down. Only two employees were there that early — my cook and a waitress who came in to mop and sweep every morning.

I went straight to my cook. Told him what happened. Asked if I could pat him down. He didn't even hesitate — said, "Go ahead." I did, checked his pockets, then asked if I could look through his car. Handed me the keys. Nothing. No money bag.

Then I went to the waitress. Told her what happened. Asked if the office manager — who was also a woman — could pat her down. She looked me dead in the eye and said, "No."

A red flag shot up.

I asked to check her car. She said, "No" again.

That's when I called the sheriff's department — because deep down, I knew. My office manager had been with me from day one. She was solid. No doubt in my mind.

When the deputies showed up, I told them everything and said straight out that I believed the waitress had taken the money. But without a warrant, there was nothing they could do.

I stood there and watched her walk out the door, get in her car, and drive off — with our $3,500.

It broke my heart.

That girl knew how hard we were working, how much blood, sweat, and time we'd poured into that place, and she still took it. It was a punch to the gut.

And that was just one story. Back then, you had to watch everything — the food, the cash, even the tools in the back. People would take whatever they could get their hands on.

But I bounced back. I had to.

And somewhere in all that chaos, I realized something.

I liked filming TV shows. More than that, I liked what they did for us. When we were on national TV, people knew we were there. They'd make the drive, just to see it for themselves.

And that's when it hit me.

If I wanted Gator Country to grow, to really make it, I had to find a way to get my own TV show — on national TV.

Looking back, that morning was a hard lesson — in trust, in grit, and in just how much it was going to take to keep this dream alive.

And then, finally, there was quiet. I sat there by myself for a moment, the rain still pounding on the roof, and I just thought, When are these storms in my life gonna stop coming?

Chapter 11
Gator 911

After that little taste of national TV on Animal Planet, I knew I had to figure out a way to use television to drive people straight down the driveway to Gator Country. But I also knew it wasn't going to work just filming the animals we already had sitting in the park. Folks could only watch me hand-feed Big Al so many times before they'd seen it all. I needed new action. I needed the wild side of the story.

That's when I put my name in for a state permit to catch nuisance alligators. These weren't zoo animals. These were gators that showed up where they weren't supposed to be—people's pools, their ponds, their backyards. They were dangerous, and people needed help. Somebody had to step in and remove them before somebody got hurt.

Problem was, there were already two guys in my area who had that permit, and to be honest, they had me over a barrel. If I wanted an alligator for my park, I had no choice but to buy from them. They'd go out, catch a nuisance gator, then turn around and charge me thirty dollars per foot just to get it. Thirty dollars a foot! That meant a ten-foot gator was costing me three hundred bucks, and there was no other way to get them legally. I couldn't keep growing the park like that. They were holding me hostage.

So I filled out the paperwork and filed for my own permit. Finally, I thought, here's my shot.

Then came the waiting. A month went by. Nothing. Another month. Still nothing. Three months passed, and not a single word. Every day I was on the phone, calling and asking about the drawing, asking about the bids. I knew how this was supposed to work—it was a sealed bid. You wrote down how much you'd pay the state per foot for the gators, sealed it, and turned it in.

Well, I already knew what I was paying those two guys—thirty bucks a foot—so I bid the same, figuring that had to be higher than anybody else. I was certain it would lock it in. But the months kept dragging on, and nothing ever happened.

Finally, I found out the truth. They hadn't redone the contract at all. They just let the good old boy system roll on, kept those same guys in year after year like it was theirs by birthright. Nobody outside their circle even had a chance.

That didn't sit right with me.

I had a good friend of mine who was a judge, a man high up in politics, and I decided it was time to pay him a visit. I hopped on a plane and flew four hundred miles to see him. When I got there, I laid it all out—every detail, every piece of paperwork, everything Texas Parks and Wildlife was doing to block me out.

The judge listened, then picked up the phone. He called the commissioner of Parks and Wildlife himself and told him I was coming. Next thing I knew, I was headed to Austin, straight to the Capitol.

I showed up with all my paperwork in hand. Sat down with the commissioner, laid it out plain as day—how the department was violating its own rules and regulations, how they weren't even holding the drawings like they were supposed to.

The commissioner looked me dead in the eye and said, "You are exactly right. Thank you for bringing this to my attention." Then he leaned in and said, "By the time you get back to Beaumont, you'll have more alligator calls than you can stand."

Well, sure enough, when I got back home, the contract was waiting. I'd won it—the whole thing. I now had the contract for the entire state of Texas for nuisance alligators.

But winning came with a price.

By going straight to the top, I'd stepped over the heads of the local game wardens. They were used to running the show, and they didn't like being bypassed.

One day, I got a call from a young game warden. Funny thing—he used to work for me back when I was at the sheriff's office. I was his sergeant; he worked under me. Now, here he was, calling me like he had the upper hand. His voice on the phone was sharp, mad. He said, "Meet me out in your front parking lot."

Something in me knew this wasn't going to be a friendly visit. Back when I worked narcotics, I always carried a tape recorder. And that day, sitting in my office at Gator Country, I felt that same old tug in my gut. I slipped that recorder into my pocket, hit record, and headed out the door.

When I stepped into the parking lot, he was already pacing, red in the face. He lit into me right off the bat. "I can't believe you went over our field captain. I can't believe you went all the way to the commissioner. You overrode all of us!" He was shaking mad.

I kept my voice calm. Told him, "Look, this wasn't personal. I just wanted a fair shot. Y'all weren't even giving me a chance at that contract."

That didn't settle him one bit. He leaned in, pointed his finger, and said, "I'll tell you what. We'll give you so many nuisance alligator calls, everybody'll be complaining on you. You won't hold that contract a year. I'll go through this park with a fine-tooth comb—permits, paperwork, you name it—and I'll bury you in it."

He just kept coming, trying to tear me down, trying to scare me into backing off.

But what he didn't know was sitting right there in my pocket. I let him finish his rant, let him stack up all his threats, then I pulled that little recorder out. Hit stop, rewound it a few seconds, and pressed play.

The look on his face changed in an instant. He knew he'd just dug his own hole. If anybody heard that tape—him, representing the State of Texas, making threats like that—it wouldn't be me in trouble.

That was the day me and Texas Parks and Wildlife came to peace.

That day, not long after the showdown with Parks and Wildlife, the calls started pouring in. Once I got that permit in my hands, the floodgates opened. I couldn't hardly sit down before the phone rang again.

One morning, I was in Vidor, Texas, at this trailer park where a deep drainage ditch cut straight through the place. That ditch was five feet deep in spots, dark and muddy, just perfect for a big gator to lay up.

The very morning before, I'd picked up the phone and called a producer out of Dallas. Her name was Melanie, and she owned a company called 12 Forward. They were in the business of making TV shows. I told her, "Look, I've got five nuisance calls lined up for the morning. It's starting to heat up, and this is before anybody else in the United States has ever done an alligator show on television." She perked up right away and told me she'd get down here as quick as she could. I said, "Well, I'll be at a trailer park in Vidor at 8 a.m., starting in a ditch. You want to see what I do, that's where I'll be." She told me she wanted to shoot what they called a "sizzle reel"—basically a sample to sell the show.

So the next morning, there I was, standing knee-deep in that ditch, water up to my chest in some spots, with my partner working a rod and reel. That's how we'd catch gators in deep water—big treble hook, heavy weight, snag 'em in the tail, then drag 'em close enough to wrestle down and rope up. Well, I'm down in this culvert, water swirling around me, when I feel something brush past my leg. Then—BAM. A pain so sharp I thought I'd been bitten. My partner's yelling, "I got him! I got him! I hooked him!" But he didn't hook the gator. He hooked me. Two out of three hooks buried right into my calf, deep.

I'm screaming at him, "You got ME, not the gator!" but at that exact moment, I feel movement between my legs. I look down, and there's a gator sliding right through, his head between my knees, his teeth scraping against my thighs. With a treble hook stuck in my leg and blood running, I shut my legs gently, reached underwater with my hands, and felt the jaw. I could feel both rows of teeth, rough like sandpaper, cold and dangerous. I knew I had one shot.

So I clamped down with my legs, shoved both hands under, and grabbed. The water exploded around me. My partner finally realized he had me hooked, not the gator, and stopped yanking. He came barreling down the bank, mud flying, to help me. Together we fought that gator, the water churning and splashing like a hurricane. Finally, we got a rope on him, rolled him over, and taped his mouth shut.

And just as I'm sitting there in the ditch, bleeding from my calf, soaked in mud, holding down a live gator, a car pulls into the parking lot. Out steps Melanie, the producer from Dallas. She gets out, eyes wide, and says, "Did I miss anything?"

She missed the whole thing.

It was a long day. By the time we finished with that first gator in Vidor, my leg was throbbing from the treble hook, but there wasn't no time to rest. Calls were stacked up. We had another three alligators to catch before sundown, and every one of them was in some mess of water or under a trailer where somebody's kids had been playing. By the end of it, I was wore out, sore, and soaked to the bone, but we had the footage Melanie needed. The cameras caught the splashes, the fights, the ropes flying, mouths being taped—it was raw, it was dangerous, it was real. That's what made the sizzle reel.

About two weeks later, my phone rang. It was Melanie. She said, "Gary, we've got a good problem… but it's still a problem." I said, "Alright, what kind of problem?" She said, "I sent the reel to A&E and CMT, and Gary, I've never seen anything move this fast in my life. We have an offer from CMT on the table already."

Now, CMT wasn't near as big as A&E. And the crazy thing was, A&E had already called too. They said they were interested, but the timing was bad—everybody was off on some kind of company retreat until Monday. They needed the weekend before they could give me an answer.

But CMT must've had someone on the inside, because that very same Friday they came back hard. They told us, "You take the deal today or we're out." Just like that. No wiggle room. They had a contract in hand, the money laid out, everything ready. They didn't want to give A&E the chance to swoop in and steal it.

So there I was—bird in the hand with CMT, or bird in the bush with A&E. And I'll tell you, it was one of the hardest decisions of my life. I didn't have no team of lawyers, no big advisors. It was just me. One decision. And I knew whichever way I went, it could change my whole life.

The pressure was heavy, but the country music folks weren't letting up. They pushed and pushed, and finally I said, "Alright. Let's do it." I signed with CMT. Just like that, I had my own TV show on national television.

And the way I found out—it couldn't have been scripted better if you tried. I was in the hospital with my daughter, sitting there while she was having surgery on her foot. My phone buzzed, and it was the call. They told me, "Gary, you've got the green light." Those words right there meant everything—I had a national TV show.

I looked at my daughter, she looked at me, and we just grabbed each other and hugged tight. We both cheered right there in that doctor's office like we'd just won the Super Bowl. Nurses, doctors, everybody around us—we told them all. It wasn't just my victory, it was ours. It was a dream come true, a feeling I can't even put in words. After all the fights, the floods, the hook in my leg, and the good old boy system trying to shut me out, I had it—my own national TV show.

They didn't waste no time once we got that green light. CMT said, "We start filming in four weeks." That's lightning fast in the TV world. They wanted ten full episodes, all done quick, because we had a small window. October and November, you can still catch alligators, but when the cold rolls in December and January, those gators go down. They bury up, they hibernate. And once they're gone, they're gone. You ain't filming nothing but empty ponds and muddy banks.

So I was staring down this contract, knowing I had to deliver ten solid episodes in less than two months. And this wasn't no staged business. Every single time that phone rang, wherever that gator was—pond, ditch, river, backyard swimming pool—we had to catch him. On top of that, I had a full film crew, eight people, $25,000 a day. Every second that camera was rolling was burning money, and every episode had to have three gators caught, no excuses. You talk about pressure—I was wound tight as a drum.

We got after it hard. Day after day, sunup to sundown, hauling equipment, cameras right in my face, producers hollering "We need more action!" while I'm knee-deep in muddy water with a rope in my hands. We fought gators in culverts, we fought them in boat slips, and I'll never forget the one that tore through a chain-link fence trying to get away. But we kept stacking episodes. Seven of them in the can before that November chill hit, and then the gators vanished like smoke.

That left three episodes undone, and the network breathing down my neck. They had already picked the air date—April 6th, 2010—and there was no moving it. We had to pick back up in March, catch three more episodes, and finish this thing. The whole winter I tried to relax, but it felt like somebody had a cinder block sitting on my chest. Every time I thought about those missing episodes, my stomach knotted up.

When March came, we hit the ground running. Calls were stacking up again, and we went after every one of them. The stress was unbelievable. I'd lay down at night and my mind would still be racing—what if the gator doesn't show? What if we miss the shot? What if the crew can't get the angle? Ten episodes or nothing.

Finally, with just two days left before that first episode was supposed to air, we landed the last gator. I can still remember the way it felt—rope went tight, mud flying, crew screaming, and then bang—we had him. We taped him up, hauled him out, and just like that, the season was done.

It was like the weight of the world slid off my shoulders. Months of pressure, millions of dollars on the line, and we did it. We had ten episodes in the bag. Now it was out of my hands.

All that was left to do was sit back and wait for April 6th, 2010. That was the night the world got introduced to my new television show on Country Music Television. The name of it was simple, straight to the point—Gator 911.

When Gator 911 hit the airwaves, Friday nights turned into something special. We'd throw big watch parties out at Gator Country, and the place would fill up fast. I'm talking hundreds of people shoulder to shoulder, eating in the restaurant, laughing, hollering every time they saw me or the crew on that big screen. The smell of fried gator tail and catfish filled the air, the bar was running wide open, and folks were cheering like it was a football game.

But the best part came the next morning. That driveway I'd worried would stay empty for so long—now it looked like an army of ants. Car after car, van after van, rolling in nonstop. Folks were coming from all over just to see the place they'd watched on TV the night before.

It was proof right there in front of me—national TV worked. The gamble, the stress, the sleepless nights, all of it—it worked for Gator Country.